catchpenny

PART ONE:
Wicked LOVER

SARAH WATHEN

Catchpenny
by Sarah Wathen

Catchpenny

ISBN-13: 978-1-942938-04-0

Cover art by Sarah Wathen
Edited by Racquel Henry
Interior design by Sarah Wathen

www.sarahwathen.com

Give feedback on the book at:
layercakeproductionsllc@gmail.com

Twitter: @SWathen_Author

First Edition
Printed in the U.S.A

part one:
wicked lover

chapter one

I stepped off the school bus, my brain still foggy and my eyes still sleepy. But when I saw the janitor re-painting my locker again, my early morning funk was slapped right off my face. Someone must have used spray paint that time, or maybe a permanent marker—not so easily cleaned as lipstick or a simple splatter of oozing garbage. My eyes scanned the lockers on either side, all faded and chipped orange paint, while mine was a bright beacon of fresh lacquer. I wondered what graffiti Henry had seen that morning on his 5 a.m. arrival to campus. Maybe just a word: "slut." Maybe something more creative, like the enormous penis, complete with pubic hair and a little squirt coming from the tip, that had been drawn on my locker door a few weeks ago. Luckily, most sharpie-wielding dipshits at my high school weren't so clever. Clever was remembered better.

It looked like Henry was almost finished covering whatever new allusion to my reputation had been left for me to find. I didn't need to guess whether or not anyone else saw the graffiti before it had been painted over—darting eyes and stifled giggles nearby told me they had. Thankful that I already had the book I needed, I changed direction, and headed for my first period class instead of my locker.

How did people even get into the school at night? I walked to class with my gaze focused straight ahead and my face expressionless. Who had I newly pissed off—and how? Whose boyfriend had been caught with his eyes glued to my ass as I passed? Or, maybe a jealous underclassman brat hadn't developed quite as well as me yet? I had been the first girl to grow breasts in grade school, years ago, and it hadn't escaped anyone's notice, no matter how baggy the shirt I wore was. Those babies just kept growing over the years, while the rest of me stretched out tall and lean. Most guys can't help but stare, and most girls hate me for it.

But I don't wear baggy shirts anymore. I pushed my shoulders back and straightened my spine, the shock and embarrassment of morning graffiti already wearing off. It never took long to remember who I was, and shrug off the ridicule of who people thought I was. Who they needed me to be. I readjusted my backpack and fluffed my hair. Screw them.

A pair of eyes locked onto mine. Tristan Jameson, Andrew Jackson's star quarterback, was walking down the hallway in my direction, staring at me. He was holding the strap of his backpack over one shoulder, the other hand in the pocket of his jeans, strolling. A half-smile played on his lips.

"Hi," he said in a low voice as he passed, so close we almost bumped shoulders.

"Hi." I glanced behind. He was looking back at me.

"Watch it!"

"Oh, sorry." I stopped short just before slamming into the oncoming student traffic. Several girls were walking together; a wall of bodies, chatting and laughing. I shot my elbows in front of me for protection, and accidentally toppled the books from one of the girl's hands.

"Why don't you look where you're going?" She stooped down to gather her things, tugging the hem of her miniskirt down and muttering under her breath.

"Here. Sorry." She snatched the book I held out for her and pushed past me with a scowl, running to catch up with the herd.

"Why don't you get a backpack?" I mumbled, watching her bustle away in the direction Tristan had been headed. He was already gone.

♠

I sat on my favorite table in the outdoor courtyard, my feet propped on the back of a conjoined concrete bench. The yard was all brick and concrete, a square space open to the sky where four school buildings met and a lone tree sprang up from a hole in the center. The tables were mostly empty, with only a few guys loitering by the doors to the cafeteria. The cafeteria was where the bulk of the student body preferred to eat. I prefer solitude. I leaned back on my hands and closed my eyes, knowing that extending my tan was hopeless so late in the season. I let the sun warm my shoulders and face, soaking it in with greed. It was the last of the summer heat, the days already shortening and the shadows lengthening into autumn.

A burst of laughter erupted nearby as a group of girls swarmed around one of the empty tables, flinging their purses and book bags on top, and my moment of peace vanished. I opened up Tolstoy's *Anna Karenina*, the pages blue after letting my closed eyes bake in the sun. I had been slogging through the book for days, and I thought once again about seeing the movie before I finished. I hate that seeing a movie changes the way a character looks in my mind, but I detest how much a movie stinks after I've already read the book. I thumbed a few pages forward to see where the chapter ended, not really in the mood for reading, but always more comfortable to have a book in hand at lunchtime.

"Meg?"

He was standing just behind me, his head cocked to one side, looking over my shoulder at the Tolstoy. I gasped—I couldn't help it.

"Hi, I'm Tristan."

He was squinting into the sun, and it was hard to tell if he was smiling or frowning.

"Yeah, I know who you are."

He shaded his eyes and laughed. Didn't everyone know who he was? He was on the billboard in front of the football field, for god's sake, his arm cocked back to throw a winning pass. *Go Bobcatts!*

"What are you reading?" His voice was soft and curious, with the hint of a Southern drawl that you didn't hear in my neighborhood. High-class molasses. He squinted to read the pages I held open in my lap.

"Uh…" I faltered. The sun shone through his light irises like glass, shocking against his dark hair. His black polo shirt was gathered loosely around one hip, the hand in his pocket pushing it up casually over the waistband of his jeans. A slice of flesh was made visible. He stood in perfect contrapposto, bookbag slung over his shoulder like Michelangelo's David holding the slingshot. I closed my book and tossed it onto the table, pretending not to notice how his jeans hung, low and delicious on slender hips. "Just something for English Lit."

"Man, that's a fat book. We never have to read stuff like that in my class."

"Aren't you a senior, too?"

"Yeah. What English class are *you* in?"

"AP," I shrugged.

"AP. What's that mean?"

"Advanced Placement."

He furrowed his brow.

"Based on college reading lists." I held up my "fat" book in illustration. "You take a test at the end and get college credits, depending on how well you do."

"Oh, wow."

I could tell he was surprised I had a brain. Most guys were. I wasn't sure what to say next, so I held his gaze, challenging him to ask me more about books.

"How can you read out here? It's so bright."

Because I'd rather read a book than sit alone with no one talking to me. "I heard that people with light eyes have a harder time adjusting to bright light."

"Really?"

He stepped closer to me, shifting his weight and putting his back to the sunlight. The color of his eyes reminded me of Halls Mentho-Lyptus cough drops after I'd sucked on one for a while and the zing got too strong to keep it in my mouth—icy blue and transparent.

"I don't want to bother you or anything," he said, dropping his voice lower, since we were face to face then. He smelled like soap and clean laundry, with something gritty underneath. Something undeniably male.

"No, I—" I cleared my throat. He was even better looking up close. "I'm not busy."

He glanced back over his shoulder and the group of girls who had been watching suddenly picked up their conversation again, all of them talking at once and fumbling with their lunches. I was waiting with as much anticipation as they had been—why on earth was he talking to me?

"I'll let you get back to your book, but I just wanted to ask you something."

"Sure. What's up?" *Those eyes.*

"Would you be my date for Homecoming this weekend?"

"Cough drop—" I spluttered.

"Huh?"

I slapped my chest and choked out a cough. "I mean…uh, the dance?"

"Yeah, the dance."

"In five days?" It was Tuesday and the dance was Saturday. I hadn't planned on going, for many reasons.

"Four. Depending on how you count it," he said, a blinding smile spreading across his face. "Today's halfway through."

"I guess it is."

"And Saturday would only be a half-day, since the dance is that night." He was daring me to accept the challenge. I could never refuse a dare, especially one with such an irresistible smile attached.

"Wait. Don't you have a girlfriend?" I wasn't exactly buddies with anyone in the popular crowd at Andrew Jackson, nowhere close. But everyone knew that the star quarterback and the head cheerleader had been together since freshman year. Sugary sweet.

"No. I don't have a girlfriend." That smile again, but with an undercurrent in his voice.

The neighboring table had gone silent once more, the bombshell news of Tristan's single status freezing them all mid-prattle.

"Absolutely." I grinned over his shoulder—a present for our shocked audience.

"Absolutely, you'll go with me?"

Did he really think I would say no? The curiosity itself was enough for me to agree.

"Sure. Why not?" I shrugged, like it was nothing to me. Yeah, right.

"Great. Okay, lemme just get your number…" He handed me his phone and I punched my number in, wondering what kind of psychedelic rabbit hole I had accidentally wandered through. Had somebody drugged my orange juice that morning? He took his phone back and saved, whispering, "Meg…Shannon," as he typed. "I'll call you, so you'll have mine."

"I don't have a cellphone. That's the number at my house."

"Oh."

I felt my cheeks getting hot, and nothing to do with the sun. Was I the only person at school without a cellphone or something?

"Okay. Well, I'll see you around, then?"

"Yeah, see ya." I resisted the urge to bite down on my knuckles.

He winked at me and waved over his shoulder as he turned back to the courtyard entrance. His jeans looked even nicer from behind, snug around his well-shaped glutes and muscular thighs. "Bye, Meg."

"Bye."

I picked my book up again, refusing to gaze at his retreating form in concert with the other females. A wink, though. What did that mean? Maybe it was just the bright light on his Mentho-Lyptus eyes. I opened *Anna Karenina* again and pretended to concentrate for the rest of lunch. But I couldn't read another word.

chapter two

I checked the clock as I rushed through the bedroom. Shit, it was already 5:45. I picked up dirty underwear and odd socks with my toes, transferring them to my hands like a monkey, before flinging them into the laundry hamper. If I let stuff lay around for more than a few hours, my tiny, overpopulated home was likely to explode into chaos that was hard to recover from. And I planned to be gone for a while that night.

I wondered if Tristan was a punctual kind of guy, and how much longer I had to obsess over household chores. My stomach was in knots; he said he'd pick me up at 6:00, though the dance didn't start until 7:00 and my place was only a few minutes from campus. That was worrisome. Either he wanted to arrive early to the dance (while I definitely preferred to show up late and leave early for most social functions) or he had a pre-dance plan. He also told me not to eat dinner, but the only restaurant in town was Big Joe's, and I hoped to god he wasn't planning to take me there in a Homecoming dress.

I paused in my frantic tidying to picture the scene: Big Joe's is your classic mountain log-cabin, Southern-country-grub-with-all-the-fixin's kind of place, and I was good friends with several people who worked in the kitchens. They had known me in cut-offs and tank tops, with dirty feet and unwashed hair, for most of my life, just like extended family. If Tristan brought me there, they would take one look at me and laugh their asses off, then ask where the real Meg Shannon was hiding. But, Big Joe's was the likeliest candidate for a pre-dance dinner date—hell, the only candidate. And anyone else Homecoming-bound, who wanted to eat out, would be there, too. Gross.

"Meg! Piper said I can only have two fish sticks and I need three," my youngest sister, Tessa, yelled from another room.

I threw down a broken toy truck totally unconcerned anymore whether filth attracted more filth. Let someone trip over it. I stomped past the living room and glared at Piper in our cramped, galley-style kitchen.

"You guys made *fish sticks*?" My nose crinkled at the rising aroma. I imagined microscopic fishy particles, detaching from the fried finger food and wafting through the air, clinging to my hair and skin. "Great. Now it's gonna smell like fish when he shows up, Piper."

She shrugged, but her shoulders were tense. She banged another tin tray into the oven. "That's all we had. You need to go grocery shopping."

"I will on mom's next payday. Just make a buttload of french fries."

"What do you think I'm doing?" she said, then in an undertone, "Thank you very much, Piper."

I wanted to strangle her, but repeated, "Thank you very much, Piper. I really appreciate you taking over today. You're amazing."

My lips pursed in forced gratitude. Like I hadn't done my share of baby-sitting, ever since I was practically a baby myself. But, I needed Piper's compliance that night, and why not let her soak up the accolades for once? I had spent most of the day in Tenakho Falls at Cassie's salon, getting the freebie cousin special. As soon as I got home I had to shower—hair pinned up, careful not to ruin my painstakingly made-up face and fresh manicure—and change into my dress. I was about to take off for the whole night and Piper would have to corral the beasts without my help. Or mom's help, of course. She was working a double shift again. Of course.

"Well. You look awesome," Piper offered, softening just a little. Her cheeks were still flushed from the heat of the kitchen and the irritation of whining siblings, but she returned my smile. I was proud of her for restraining her jealousy; Piper loved to dress up and she would have killed to go to the dance, but no one had asked her and she wasn't the type to go stag. "I can't believe Cassie got your hair to do that."

She motioned to my ringlet curls, as shocked as I was by how well my hair was behaving. I had earned the nickname "Afro" at a young age because of my normally bushy, unruly mane. I usually just tried to keep it out of my face in a ponytail, or tamed into a thick braid, but Cassie works miracles. Smooth locks cascaded over my shoulders in artful spirals. When I left the salon, she shoved two bottles into my hands—a "curl enhancer" and a "frizz eliminator"—and made me promise to use them every day. Like I wanted my hair to be a big poof ball? Of course I would use the stuff, now that I knew what it could do. The right haircut helped, too. Thank god for generous, salon-owning cousins.

A soft knock.

"Oh no." I looked towards the front door, anxious and elated. "He's early."

"Why are you wringing your hands? You look ready," said Piper.

"I am."

"Don't worry, I got this. Get outta here."

"Thanks." I swooped in for a hug, suddenly overcome with affection for my sister. She did have it, I could trust her. Piper squeezed into the embrace and I shoved away. "Don't get all mushy on me. Cassie will kill me if I wreck her make-up job."

Piper wiped a tear and I almost killed her. I gave her a warning look, before twirling away in the other direction to retrieve my purse from the bathroom.

"Well, you're graduating soon. I'll miss you, is all," she called after me.

I had almost a whole year before I graduated, and for me it seemed like an eternity. I stuffed my lipstick and compact into the glittery handbag and hurried back through the house. My little brother scurried underfoot and I nearly went sprawling. "Charlie, watch out."

"Meg, wait."

"What? I'm in a hurry, sweetie." I heard the whine in my tone with a measure of shame. I hate whiners.

"I just wanted to tell you that you look like a princess."

Seeing his honest, innocent face, I stopped in my tracks and squatted down so that my face was on his level. "Thank you, Charlie Brown. Piper, what kind of princess movies have you been showing him?"

My sister walked into the living room with a knowing smile, wiping her hands on a kitchen towel. "The Great Gatsby. He thinks all the pretty ladies at the big parties are princesses."

I snorted in surprise, nearly blowing snot from my nose at the irony. I was even further away from being a chick in the Great Gatsby than I was from being a princess. "Those are just rich people, Brownie." I ruffled his hair as I stood up and swooshed my arms in front of me in an everybody-out-of-my-way gesture.

"I love you, Meg," said my littlest sister, Tessa, appearing waist-side.

But I didn't have time for any more touchy-feelies. I nodded and held my finger to my lips as I neared the front door.

Tessa whispered, "I know. We're not here."

I mouthed, "Good girl," then I cracked open the door, slipped out, and shut it behind me in an instant, hoping to leave the fishy smell behind.

"Hello, Tristan."

He was facing away from the door with his hands locked behind his back, one of them holding a plastic box. I tried to get a look at what was inside it, but he turned around when he heard my voice, in a tailored black tuxedo with a dark red vest and tie. His eyebrows shot up over those bright blue eyes when he saw me, and he scanned me from head to toe.

He chuckled softly, but said nothing.

I put a hand on my hip and let him take it all in; I knew I looked hot and I was never shy about that kind of attention. My brother was actually closer than I gave him credit for when he compared me to a Gatsby girl. I had acquired a smashing hand-me-down from my cousin, Debra; a blood-red, slinky flapper dress from the 1920's. I wasn't an expert on antique apparel, but it looked authentic to me and had obviously been handed down a dozen times. Judging by the amount of original fabric it had left, the dress also been altered almost as often, but it was nothing I couldn't handle touching up again. I started sewing as soon as I was old enough to be embarrassed by my shabby thrift store wardrobe. My clothes may be old and used, but I know how to freshen something up so it fits like a glove. The flapper dress was a pretty tight glove, I knew. I'm taller and bustier than Debra, and so the finished effect of my most recent alterations made a shorter, more revealing shift than most flapper girls would have been comfortable wearing.

Tristan still hadn't said anything.

Okay, so my tits were kinda pouring out, I had to confess, following his eyes with a smirk. Oh well, I like mesmerizing guys. Especially guys that looked like Tristan Jameson.

"You look…" he started.

"Don't act so surprised or you might start to hurt my feelings." My feelings were in no danger of being hurt; I had figured out soon enough why he asked me to the dance. It wasn't hard to catch snippets of gossip in a small town, especially when people purposely talked loud enough for me to hear. In the few days I had to prepare for the dance—in a frenzy of sewing and calling in favors from family members—I also had ample opportunity to prepare for my supposed role. Word in the halls and bathroom stalls: the quarterback was dying to get laid and his girlfriend wasn't putting out. But, I was already used to the "Meg Shannon's a sure thing," rumors.

"I'm sorry." He snapped out of his momentary daze. "Beautiful just didn't seem to be a good enough word."

"Oh. Er..."

He just kept staring at me.

"Stunning?" I offered.

"Well, yeah. I guess that's better," he admitted, regaining composure and flashing me a smile. "You are stunning."

"Thanks." My laugh sounded tinny and thin.

"Don't thank *me*." He stepped through the comfort zone, close enough that our noses could've touched if I leaned in, and so suddenly intimate that

I felt my cheeks grow hot. I hadn't noticed how white his teeth were—they almost rivaled the brightness of his eyes. It was my turn to feel stunned as he curled one of my ringlets around his finger.

Oh…

A grin split his face, inches from mine, my discomposure obvious. He was showing me up. I guess I had sort of baited him. He ran a knuckle over my beaded antique headband (which Cassie insisted completed the Roaring '20's look), then leaned in and gave me a soft peck on the forehead.

"Lovely would work, too," he whispered.

I narrowed my eyes. He knew how gorgeous he was and he knew what he did to girls, without a doubt. I felt like an idiot and out of my league, suddenly unsure of whether I was up to the challenge after all.

"So." He straightened up and glanced over my shoulder at the front door, and I knew that the polite move would be to invite him inside.

I wasn't going to do that, etiquette be damned. "So?"

"Doesn't your mom want to take pictures, Meg?"

Pictures.

I hadn't thought about pictures. Was he serious? Would his mom be expecting to share snapshots with my mom? The thought was ludicrous. My mother wasn't into stuff like that, especially with the likes of Stephanie Jameson, PTA president and Bobcatt enthusiast.

"She's at work."

"Oh. Where does she work?" A polite question.

"The hotel."

"By the interstate? What does she do there?" He cocked his head to the side, as if he really wanted to know.

"She's a maid," I said flatly. Were we done with polite, yet? I let the uncomfortable moment linger.

His eyes darted to my shoulder. "Is that chocolate?"

"Huh?" His hand shot up to wipe a brown smear from my skin with one finger. I felt the blood drain from my face, mortified. "Damn it, Charlie. I'm sorry, let me get you something to clean that off with…"

"Forget it." He popped his finger into his mouth. "Hazelnut."

I stared at him, remembering my brother's grubby, chocolate-coated fingers. Did he have any idea where those fingers roam all day long? "That doesn't gross you out?"

He shrugged, "I have a little sister who loves chocolate, too."

"Oh." It was kind of disgusting, but I loved it. That was the last thing I would have expected from a guy like Tristan. But really, I had no idea what he was like at all. Intriguing.

"This is for you," he said, unaware of the impression his humble chocolate scavenging had made. He opened the little plastic box; it held a corsage of deep red roses. "I don't think I can pin it anywhere…"

"Um, yeah it's…enormous."

We both laughed, as he made a show of searching for a wide enough stretch of fabric on the bust-line of my dress, ducking low to inspect all sides and shaking his head, helpless. The corsage was huge, the fabric of my dress tiny. I took the roses and placed them right on top of my breasts, which were high enough in a push-up bra to be a nice table for them. "Are you trying to cover me up?"

"That would be a crime." He stepped back and appraised me in illustration. "Although I think maybe my mom had that in mind, now that I see it on you."

"Maybe…" I left out the obvious. His mom probably hadn't been happy that her golden boy was taking me to the dance, rather than his re-portedly prim and proper ex-girlfriend. The rumors had probably reached Mom, and she may have suspected I'd wear something skimpy. I *had*, so I couldn't really take offense to that. More likely, though, she thought I'd need some dressing up. Now that was offensive.

"My mom, jeez. She's a little too into this stuff."

"I'll show her."

I pulled one of the buds from its nest of greenery and baby's breath and snapped my teeth around the stem, determined to make a joke of it. I did my best at a bobcat growl.

"Or, we can prune it down a little, and there'd still be plenty left," I said.

Another rose went into the band at my temple.

"Don't mess up your hair." His brows knitted and his smile gone, he took the rose from my headband, then smoothed my locks back into place.

We got quiet.

My eyes found his boutonniere, already inserted into his lapel expertly. So, his mother had supplied *his* roses, too. How was she such a part of our date when she wasn't even there? I wasn't sure whether to feel creeped out or thankful.

"I forgot to get you a boutonniere anyway." I motioned to his im-maculate tux, aware that I hadn't yet complimented him. "You look very nice, by the way."

"Thank you."

He ran fingers through his dark hair, almost as black as his jacket, then flashed me the famous billboard smile. That reminded me how far he was out of my league, and I told the butterflies in my stomach to calm down. *Do not fall for the god damn star quarterback, you idiot insects.*

"And look," he said, taking the corsage from me and bringing my hand to his lips in one fluid motion. He slipped the flowers over my hand and stroked the inside of my wrist with his thumb.

"Oh." I looked down at our intertwined hands. "A bracelet band. How ingenious." At least he knew what to do—knew it like he'd read the manual. The whole corsage thing was foreign to me, but of course he'd given out more than a few.

He half-turned and offered me his elbow, "Shall we?"

A loud wail sounded from inside, followed by a sharp smack, and then Piper's muffled warning. The "we're not here" charade had met its end. I put my flower-free hand in his arm and urged him away from the front door before anything more embarrassing happened. "Definitely. Let's go."

chapter three

As soon as we rounded the corner of the Shannon Family trailer, a stretch limousine came into view. I marveled at the juxtaposition.

"Nice ride."

"Just borrowing it," he said with a wink.

There was that wink again. What did it mean and why did I feel it in my thighs?

A shirtless old man sat on his stoop next door, glaring at us, with a lit cigarette dangling from his lips. I waved. His pit bull growled next to him on a chain. I tried to seem nonchalant and keep my stiletto heels from plunging into the dirt. A hulking driver stood by the limo like a bodyguard, and he opened the door as we approached.

"Barney, I told you I wanted to do that," Tristan said under his breath, as the big man bent a little at the waist in my direction.

I was impressed that this Barney was professional enough to keep his eyes off my chest, but I noticed the stifled humor at the corners of his mouth. Tristan sighed, irritated, and then softened his expression for me as he held out his hand to help me into the cab.

The inside was cool when I stepped in. It was spacious, all cream-colored leather and chrome, with couch-style seats lining most of the walls under heavily tinted, panoramic windows. The open central area was carpeted in luxurious charcoal gray, with a small sideboard across from the door that looked like it served as a bar and storage cabinet. There was a remote control on the table, and music playing quietly in surround speakers. Country music. I'd have to fix that; there's nothing grosser, musically speaking. Living in a small Appalachian town where it was ubiquitous was tough on the ears. I flopped down on the comfy leather seat next to the sideboard and was messing with the remote before Tristan closed the doors.

"Satellite radio, awesome." It was a rare luxury for me. Cassie had one at the salon, but she wouldn't let me tamper with it during shop-open hours. She kept it on some kind of pop hits station to please the average customer until the doors were locked. Forgetting my gorgeous date for a second, I flipped through dozens of stations. Lots looked interesting but inappropriate. Alternative Rock? A country music boy probably wouldn't like that. A comedy station wasn't the right fit. Howard Stern, no. NPR, nope. "Ah, this is good."

Vivaldi tinkled through the cabin and I smiled to myself about my brother's earlier princess remark. Princesses probably listened to Celtic Lutes or Gregorian monks chanting in the fairy tales, but Vivaldi set the scene just fine.

Tristan was dubious. "Classical?"

"Classical is better for the occasion, don't you think?" I motioned to our wardrobes and our lush surroundings, then waved my hand in front of me as if I was holding an imaginary lace handkerchief or some other dainty nonsense. He caught my mocking fingers and pressed his lips to the top of my hand. Soft and warm. I had been wondering how those full lips would feel, but I didn't think I'd find out so quickly. I batted my eyelids like it was a joke. Except it wasn't.

"Whatever you like," he said, settling onto the seat next to me. "You seriously like this stuff, though?"

"Hell yeah. You can check out tons of classical CD's at the library, and they never have any scratches since no one ever listens to them. Plus, Mozart's good for studying."

He cocked his head. "Is it?"

"The best."

The two hours I get every school night to study goes much more smoothly if I can block out all the household melodrama with noise-canceling headphones—which I also borrow from the library. My mom never even graduated from high school, and she says she wants more for her oldest daughter. She knows she can't really give me much but a rigorous work ethic. But, hey work ethic is great for studying. She insists that my chance in life lay in my intellect and she's always strictly enforced study time. That rule works fine for me, since I've been saddled with mothering four younger siblings since before Kindergarten. It's the only chance I get to be blissfully unencumbered at home.

"Oh, speak of the devil—this one's Mozart," I said, as the next tune swelled into *Symphony 35*.

"Why is Mozart good for studying?"

"Helps you concentrate." I closed my eyes to illustrate. After the song was half-over, I opened my eyes and saw him watching me. "What?"

"You look...peaceful."

"Do I?" Funny. Peaceful wasn't how I felt at that moment at all.

"I think I like Mozart now, too."

I closed my eyes again and smiled inside. He was admiring me. I could almost feel his gaze. The violins rose and fell, trilling and swooping. Soaring. I tried to keep my breathing as steady as the deep cello base notes, but my pulse quickened with the crescendo, knowing he was watching me. I could hear Tristan's hushed breathing next to me, and I felt him sink further into the cushions, his shoulder rubbing against mine.

"Does it work?" he asked, once the symphony came to a close.

"Work?" I had been trying not to think; trying to sit there and look pretty, and not think about how much I liked him watching me like that.

"For studying."

"Seems to work for me." I sat up, feeling a little...dreamy. Guys never ask me about my grades. What should I say? "My grades are pretty good, I guess." I was almost straight-A.

He groaned. "Mine aren't."

"I can help you with your homework, if you want," I smirked.

"Really?"

"Oh yeah, I have some pretty good study techniques I can share with you." It was hard to hold in my laughter. The irony of him being my study buddy was too much.

"Thanks," he said, frowning.

He wasn't getting the joke. "And S.A.T.'s are coming up. I already took it for practice last year, so I can give you a few tips."

"I haven't even thought about the S.A.T.'s yet."

"Well, you're in trouble," I sang, shaking my head and looking down at my hands.

"So, you already took it?"

"Yeah. I did okay, but I want a better score, so I'm gonna re-test." I watched his face turn down in worry and I patted his thigh, "Don't worry, we'll get you through it."

"Good, thanks."

He was honestly asking me to study with him. He seemed so genuine. I had left my hand on his thigh, perplexed, and he covered it with his own. Then he leaned in.

"Homework later. First..." His face was so close to mine that I could smell his skin. Aftershave, something spicy and crisp. My eyelids closed and I felt my lips parting like they had a will of their own. I was more than ready to taste him, too. But he moved past my lips and whispered in my ear, "Champagne."

I blinked. Genuine, indeed. *Bah!*

He winked at me—the jerk—as he rose, crouching low in the cabin to kneel by the side table. He opened a hidden cabinet beneath and pulled out first a bag of ice, which he emptied into an ice bucket set into the table, then a bottle of bubbly.

"Where'd you get that?" I looked behind me to check that the window through to Barney was closed. "That window mirror's not one-way is it?"

"Like he can see us, but we can't see him? Nah," he shook his head, returning with the bottle and two red plastic cups. "I already checked."

"Okay, well if you're sure..."

"I'm sure." He popped the cork and poured slowly, letting the fizz settle, while I peered through the side windows around us. We were on a pretty lonely road, not hard to find in Shirley. But Shirley was a dry county, added to the fact that we were underage. I wondered whether drinking in a limo was considered against an "open container" law. Yet, since alcohol was more illegal on so many other points at that moment, it didn't seem to matter. Did the fact that Tristan's father was the town sheriff make it easier or harder for him to break the rules? Was he being dangerous to impress me, or would his dad simply lose any paperwork that happened to cross his desk about his son? Having never been on the other side of the law before, I had no idea. But I liked the thrill and I'd never tasted champagne.

"Sorry, the plastic cups aren't so romantic," he said, handing mine over.

"Actually...I think it's very romantic." I shrugged, feeling shy. I wasn't used to that kind of treatment from guys. Champagne, wow.

He clinked his cup against mine, the plastic sounding more like a dull tap. "To a promising night, full of new possibilities."

I felt my eyes widen and my eyebrows raise, as I took a sip. "And where'd you get *that?*"

He laughed. "The toast?"

"The champagne and the toast."

"My older sister came home from college for the Homecoming weekend. She set me up."

"That was very nice of her..." I left my comment open, hoping he'd continue with some kind of explanation to our odd date.

"She just wants the night to go smoothly."

I waited. Then, couldn't resist, "Why?"

Tristan shrugged and looked out the window. "It's a celebration. Ashley's no good for me, and Liza—my sister—she's the one who helped me see that."

Well, it was good to get that out of the way. But I wasn't sure what to say.

Tristan took in a huge breath and let it out. "Huh. That felt good to admit."

He looked at me, perplexed.

"So. That's all fine and good, but I have to say I was surprised when you asked *me.*"

His face split into an ironic grin, but his eyes were serious. "You're the most interesting girl at school."

"Interesting?" I folded my arms and raised an eyebrow, hoping my look would force him to the truth. I was trying to bait him, make him admit that he had asked me to the dance so that I would sleep with him afterward.

"A lot more interesting than Ashley, I can tell already." He exhaled loudly and leaned forward with his elbows on his knees. He shook his head and scrubbed his scalp with his fingers, like frustration was mounting just thinking of her.

Whoa. A change of subject was in immediate order. I didn't want to discuss exes either and the bubbly was heating up my knees. "Well anyway, you told me not to eat dinner. Did you just want to get me drunk, Tristan?"

He smiled and let his shoulders fall. "No. I have a surprise for you."

"Another one?"

He went to the magic cupboard again, saying, "We don't have many fine dining options around here—"

"Many?"

"I mean, no fine dining options. So I thought we could eat here."

"Here?"

"Yep." He brought out a picnic-backpack and sat on the carpeted flooring next to my feet, then pulled out plates, utensils, and linen napkins. Next: a small cutting board and a knife. "I wasn't sure what you'd like, so I thought variety would be good."

"Liza thought," I corrected.

"Yeah."

"I like this sister of yours." I watched him dig out cheeses, meats, spreads, and pre-sliced fruit in little containers, placing them around himself on the floor and leather seat. He was just the cutest, sniffing the items as he brought them out, probably as unsure of what awaited us as I was. He dropped one of the containers and a grape escaped and rolled against my shoe. He apologized and wiped my high heal with his napkin. How could someone look so clumsy and so gorgeous at the same time?

"You know, you're very different than what I expected."

"What do you mean?" He paused in his mobile fine dining operation to look up at me.

"You just always seemed like such an asshole when I saw you from a distance," I blurted. "But you're a really nice guy."

"An asshole?"

"I mean, before I really met you."

He looked at me, his pretty face scrunched confusion but the corner of his mouth turned up in a smile. He returned to his task. "Maybe you shouldn't judge people before you meet them."

He said it without a hint of resentment; it was probably just something he'd heard repeated all his life. But it felt like a slap in the face to me, however gentle. Why should I think his personality sucked, just because he was beautiful? I had always thought of myself as open-minded and accepting, the least judgmental person I knew. How wrong I was about Tristan, and maybe myself, too.

He had started slicing pepperoni on the cutting board and my mouth began to water. I was so ready to let down my guard. "This looks like the best celebration feast I've ever seen. Gimme some, I'm starving."

While he sliced off pieces of cheese and hard sausage, buttered fresh buns, and placed them on the plate in my lap, we chatted about nothing in particular and commented on Liza's taste in food. We agreed that one of the cheeses was too stinky and the liver-mousse-thing was just nasty. Tristan chucked both out the window. The prosciutto stuff was mouth-watering and the grapes were so sweet that we fought over the last one. Barney meandered through the back mountain roads. Shirley County bordered a National Forest to the south, and we wandered in and out of it, along tranquil, deserted roads. Tristan asked about what was playing on the classical station now and again, and I supplied information where I could, but there was way too much material for me to recognize it all.

"A harvest moon," I gasped, when I glanced out the window through a clearing in the trees. Were we already that late into autumn? I crawled across the seats to the front of the cabin and rapped on the divider window. "Barney, stop for a minute."

"What's up?" Tristan slammed the rest of his champagne and motioned to mine. He tucked the empty bottle into the backpack as I felt the limo slow and pull onto the gravel shoulder.

"Shit, I didn't think about the champagne. Sorry." My words slurred and my tongue already felt thick; I knew I couldn't drink the rest of mine in one gulp, so I handed it to him and he hid it in the cabinet.

"S'okay, what's goin' on?"

I grabbed his arm, craning my neck for a better view. "The moon. I have to see it—it's huge."

chapter four

As soon as I pushed the door open I recognized where we had stopped: my old stomping grounds from when I was grubby-footed, tangle-haired kid. It was a perfect outlook, where the road bordered a sheer cliff face. The slice of sky was sublime, the view of Shirley Valley below breathtaking.

"Beautiful," I murmured, heading towards the edge, magnetized to the moon as surely as the tides. I felt my heels sink into the dirt and I was done with those shoes. I slipped both of them off and threw them back into the cab, narrowly missing Tristan as he got out.

"Good arm," he said, and whistled in appreciation.

"Thanks," I called back over my shoulder, momentarily free. My toes had been pinched in those things for over an hour and the dirt felt good between my toes.

Tristan picked up his pace behind me. "Careful, you're really close to the edge."

I shot him a look full of arrogance. Valley boys visited the mountains, but they never played there. "Please."

A narrow column of rock jutted up from the valley, separated from the main cliff by about two feet. We had always called it the exclamation point (or just "the point" for short) when I was a kid, because that's exactly what it looked like. It was the first and smallest of the buttes, as the valley below met the canyons, and the mountains on either side squeezed the land into a bottleneck, with violent rapids rushing below. The point was wide enough for a couple people to sit on, maybe four people to stand on carefully. I hopped out onto the column of stone, my bare toes gripping the stone when I landed, steady and sure. I'd done it a million times. I focused on the moon; it looked as big as a planet about to crash right into the earth. A yellow sphere of Swiss cheese, in planetary proportions.

"The wolves will be out in force tonight," I said, then threw my head back in a long howl. A prompt response echoed in the distance, the owner of which was more likely a hound dog hunting with his master than a roaming wolf. I laughed and looked back to see my date turning green behind me. "Don't worry, I've got good balance—my mom says I've always been a mountain goat."

He shook his head, sizing me up from the rear. "More like a mountain lion. Please come back, though."

He held out his hand, obviously closer to the rim than he was comfortable with, but I ignored it. I turned back to the moon. "It's not full yet."

"Looks pretty full to me."

"No, it's still waxing. It'll be full tomorrow."

"Want to bet?" He stuck his hand out further, daring me to accept a shake on it.

"Okay. I know I'm right."

The instant my hand made contact with his, his grip turned to iron and he yanked me towards himself, off the point and across the chasm. I crashed into his chest and he moved backwards with me—solid, not stumbling. His arms wrapped around my shoulders like steel girders, his body immovable and his face unflinching.

"You're dangerous," he mumbled, eyes blazing.

I tried to say, "You should talk," but I'd somehow lost my voice.

"Away from the sheer drop."

"Okay." I nodded, glad to finally produce a sound with my startled vocal chords. I let him thread his fingers through mine, and he led me back to the car.

In the safety of the limo, he lounged back onto the seat, his eyes smoldering as he watched me. I settled myself opposite, arranging the beads of my cocktail dress and fluffing my curls, not really sure what had just occurred between us. Maybe he was angry with me; he sure looked it. I said, as innocently as I could manage, "Are you afraid of heights?"

"Afraid of having to dive off a cliff to catch you, maybe."

I snorted. "Right."

"Reckless," he sighed, shaking his head.

"Sorry…"

"Sorry? You're not like any girl I've ever met, Meg. It's a lot to take in, but there's no reason to be sorry."

I fumbled with my beads a little more, unsure of how to proceed. I felt the car start to roll and I looked up in reaction, to see a door in the ceiling just over Tristan's head. I had an idea. "Hey, we can get a perfect view of the moon from in here. That's a sunroof, right?"

He looked above his head and his expression cooled. "Actually, I've been wanting to try that ever since I first got in."

"You mean...ejector seat?" I met his spreading grin and he nodded, then reached over to push a button by his armrest. The window in the ceiling slid open and Tristan grabbed my hand, pulling me over to crouch with him on the seat below the skylight.

"Ejector seat!" we yelled together, springing up through the open roof, him laughing and me cheering like a five-year-old. The sky spread over us like velvet lavender, a blanket of winking stars around the glowing lunar orb. It felt so close I wanted to reach up and touch it—moments like that are the closest I ever get to church.

We watched the sky together in silence. I slid my eyes in Tristan's direction and saw his own closed, his face content. The air was getting cooler, twilight fading into night, and I shivered as Barney picked up speed. My hair started to whip around my face and I grabbed as much of it as I could in one hand to save the ringlets, gripping the roof with the other. I wondered if my "frizz eliminator" would hold up to such abuse, and I squeezed eyelids shut against the wind and frenzy of escaping curls. Strong fingers encircled my wrist, pulling it down and trapping it behind my waist. My eyes snapped open and found him so close I could feel the tickle of his cheek against mine. My hair whirled around us like a tornado.

His voice was deep and urgent in my ear. "Don't put your hair back."

"It'll be an afro in a minute."

"I like it wild. I like *you* wild."

I turned a fraction and my lips brushed against his. His eyes watched my mouth. "Kiss me, Tristan."

He cupped my face with his hands, so large and warm I felt my cool cheeks blaze instantly, but so gentle he was barely touching me. He looked at me and hesitated, holding my gaze as if he were about to say something first, his face close enough I swear I could feel a spark between our lips. I couldn't wait another second. I found the heat of his mouth and slid my hands inside his jacket and around his waist. He answered me, caution forgotten along with the moon. Was that him who moaned in relief or me? I couldn't tell, melted together as we were. As one.

Both our knees gave way and I felt myself collapsing onto the seat below, then toppling to the floor. His arms were around my shoulders and under my thighs, catching our fall in an expert roll. He landed on top, hovering over me and devouring my neck while I locked my ankles around his back. His lips were as soft as his body was hard, and I felt an electric zing at every point where we connected. All thoughts of preserving my pristine Homecoming costume faded into the smell of his skin, the taste of his mouth, and the hills and valleys of his body. I blended into the texture of him.

"Meg, you're doing it again," a little naggy voice reminded me in my head. I was losing myself, losing control. Again. *"What kind of girl gives it up in a limo on the way to the dance? I mean, you haven't even finished the date yet, dummy."*

"I don't care."

"Don't care about what," Tristan said between kisses, his voice husky.

I'd said that out loud? I sat back in a daze, trying to catch my breath and focus. How was I suddenly on top? I looked down and saw the glare of streetlights on Tristan's face and realized we were heading back into town. Towards school. Towards the dance. My dress was pushed up around my hips, silk panties dark red against black tuxedo pants. At least he had controlled himself; his pants were still zipped.

Wait a minute. I did care what I looked like at that damned dance. I did want to retain the carefully crafted princess veneer that Cassie summoned like magic, and that my little brother adored. And I wanted to look beautiful on Tristan's arm.

I looked out the window and tried to regain my bearings. "I think we're almost there."

"Oh...okay," he panted. "Alright, I'm sorry."

"What are you sorry about? I was the one acting like an animal," I chuckled, sort of embarrassed. I spotted the Bobcatts billboard with Tristan as the model, that classic smile pasted on his perfect face. Then I looked down at him, still pinned under my satiny crotch, and saw that face twisted in frustration.

"Poor guy, I'll help you with that." I know a few tricks to relieve a boy's frustration in two minutes flat, and Tristan deserved it that night already. I smiled, thinking of it as an appetizer. I stretched across the seat and reached my arm up to knock on the divider window. "Barney, once around, please."

Tristan gasped when I unzipped his fly, and I listened for more—I love when boys make fun sounds. Afterwards, I straightened up and patted his pretty cheek affectionately. As I tamed my hair and considered that applying more lipstick would be a good idea, I caught the glazed-over look on Tristan's face. He lay like a puddle of Jell-O, staring at the ceiling and not bothering to fix his pants.

"Come on, Tristan. Don't tell me that was your first BJ?"

"Are you kidding?" His voice was hoarse. "Ashley made me get down on my knees with her and pray for forgiveness, after what her dad called heavy petting."

He must've been be joking. I laughed, but he didn't. Oh, god. He wasn't joking. "Er…how humiliating."

"Yeah." He didn't seem embarrassed, though—more like enlightened.

Praying after a little boob squeeze. Was that really what other girls did? Surely Ashley was an exception. I didn't know what to say. I wasn't religious, but I didn't care if someone else was, as long as they didn't involve me. Was Tristan religious? I tested the spiritual climate, "Forcing someone to pray is kinda sick."

"That's what Liza said." His breath was coming fast, like he'd been gifted with an epiphany. He sat up, tucking his shirt in and straightening his tuxedo vest. "She said Ashley's been controlling my heart through my… dick." He paused, looking abashed at the word. I smoothed away my smile with an effort. "Like I'm her puppet. Or something."

I resisted the urge to shake my head in disgust. How long had they dated? Since Freshman year, until right before he asked me to the dance. So, four years. That sucked. Fourteen through eighteen, if Tristan already had a birthday that year (I had already turned eighteen). He had all those hormones raging just as mine were, and I was hard-pressed to resist them. The idea that guys are more into sex than girls is a myth.

I didn't understand girls like Ashley, pretending to have no passion of their own and always fending the boys off. Chicks like her made it harder for honest, sexually liberated young women like me to be myself. The logic made no sense: in our culture, boys are allowed—no, *expected*—to be "virile" and "hot-blooded." But who the hell are they supposed to sow their wild oats with? Not nice girls. Girls who had sex with boys were "sluts."

Like me, according to the rumor. One of my favorites was the joke that, "Meg Shannon will sleep with anyone, just to spend the night in a house other than her own." I'd been called much worse than "slut," too. I had gotten used to the nickname but I'd never own it. I like sex as much as any guy I've ever met, maybe more. Why should I be ashamed of that, just because I'm female? Hasn't our society moved past such medieval thinking? Not in Shirley County. It was like everyone was playing some game that I didn't understand the rules to. It made me want to scream and beat at my head like Rainman. No, beat nice girls' heads.

But I didn't say any of that aloud, like a catty nice girl might. I sighed and glanced at my date, all buttoned and zipped back together and sitting quietly, bemused. I remembered how anguished he had looked minutes before. Tristan had obviously been administered more than his share of the crazy, too, only in a different kind of dose. Maybe he wasn't playing the game, either.

"What's wrong with feeling good, and making someone else feel good at the same time?" I finally asked.

His eyes locked on mine, and for a second I sensed something else there. Sadness? No, resentment. "I don't know."

"I'm glad you listened to your sister," I said. "She seems pretty smart."

"She is, yeah. Well, smarter since she went to college," he said, smiling easily again. "Oh. We're here."

chapter five

My heart fell just a little; he was right, we were parked. I was so absorbed in my thoughts (and I guessed Tristan was too) that I hadn't noticed Barney's hulking shadow against the glass.

My palms started sweating, thinking about what was in store for me inside. Sometimes people were aggressive and sometimes they left me alone. Mostly, they just shit on me behind my back. Would things be better or worse for me, with Tristan by my side? My steadily growing desire to have Tristan "by my side" was making me uneasy, too.

I sighed, resigned. "Let's do this."

He pulled the handle and stepped outside, blocking Barney with his body and offering me his hand. Barney nodded at us and chuckled in a deep baritone, "Good luck, kid."

I bit my lip to keep from smiling at Tristan's sour puss after that remark, but he regained his swagger in seconds. He took my hand and tucked it into the crook of his arm, knowing I was nervous. But it was one more day at the gym for him, one more easy social event where he was widely adored. We fell in with several other pairs of dates making their way to the doors of the gymnasium, and my eyes darted all around—jittery as a squirrel—trying to recognize anyone friendly. The crowd thickened as we got closer, and I peered ahead and saw the reason for delay; the double doors were decked out with dozens of balloons and partially blocked by a welcome board on an ornate brass tripod. I couldn't really see what was on the tripod, but everyone slowed down to rubberneck as they passed it. Tristan greeted friends or acquaintances here or there as we slowly made our way to the doors. Everyone wanted to be close to him. His fingers started twitching on top of my hand as bodies moved aside and my line of vision cleared. It was my turn to rubberneck.

There in front of me was a poster-size photo of Tristan and Ashley, standing together on a makeshift stage, the football field peeking through on either side. Ashley wore a sparkling tiara and held an armful of red roses over her cheerleading uniform. She was grinning and sobbing at the same time, wiping a tear and gazing up at Tristan. He was staring straight ahead, stone-faced. Still in his football gear, he had two smears of eye black on his cheeks and a sheen of sweat on his brow, under a silver, jewell-studded crown.

My eyes shot to his. "You're the freaking Homecoming King, Tristan?" I hissed.

His gaze was wary. "I should have told you."

"Oh, you think?"

"Does that bother you?" He winced as he said it. "It just happened last night, at half-time. You didn't go to the game, I guess."

"Nope," I said, trying to pull my hand from his arm, but he held onto my fingers in a vice grip.

"Come on, it's just a plastic crown," he murmured in my ear, shifting my hand so that he held me more firmly by his side.

"It's so much more than that."

"No it's not."

We moved through the doors and the vestibule roared into my consciousness, friends talking at high volume, music echoing out of the main gymnasium, and a flash from the professional photographer who was set up right beside the front doors. I blinked hard, momentarily blinded by the glare. There was a couple standing arm in arm, posing next to a column supporting a "2014" foam cutout, painted in glitter.

"Hey, Pretty-Boy!"

"See, I told you. Tristan's always on time."

I swiveled around to see a massive linebacker, Will Bartlett, bustling through the crowd with a petite blonde hanging on.

"Hey, Meg," he said as they drew nearer, and I saw the blonde elbow him in the ribs with a sneer. He turned to her, confused. "What?"

Oh, not allowed to talk to me anymore, huh? I looked at them both, impassive. There was no reason to start a fight. Of course, Will would be receiving no more help from me on his anatomy labs. We had been lab partners since the beginning of the year and he leaned on my superior skills with a scalpel and my ability to read instructions to get him passing grades. I didn't mind, since he was always nice to me—nice to everyone, probably. But, who would expect him to stand against that prissy trophy girlfriend he had on his arm? Nope, he would let her corral him to the dark side, I was sure of it.

"On time for what?" asked Tristan, oblivious to the exchange.

"For the first dance with Ashley, of course," said the blonde, her fist on her hip. "They're waiting to announce you guys—she's already backstage, come on."

"There's nothing to announce, Shelly," he groaned. "Why would I dance with her?"

"Because you're Bobcatt King and Queen, *Tristan,*" Shelly said with a scowl. "It's just one dance."

Will looked back and forth between them, keeping silent and avoiding my eyes.

"I don't care. I'm here with Meg. Ashley and I broke up—you know that."

"Don't be an asshole, Tri—"

"Hey." I couldn't help myself. He was only mine for the night, sure, but nobody was going to verbally abuse my date. I grabbed his arm and hauled him off to the side, ignoring Shelly's glare. "Look, it's no big deal. I don't mind. Just come and find me afterwards, okay?"

He closed his eyes and gritted his teeth. I wondered what he was thinking, as emotions played over his face. My stomach tightened at the thought of him dancing with someone else and I reminded myself to get a grip. "It's just a formality. Get it over with and it's done," I said, then watched Shelly over Tristan's shoulder as I rested my hand against his cheek. Her frown deepened and my hand twitched with an urge to slap the hate off her cute little face. "Right?"

"Right," he said, his voice even again. He opened his eyes and smiled. "Thank you, you're right."

"See? Deep breaths." I laughed.

"You're sure you don't mind?" His fingers grazed my wrist, found my elbow. "I'm *your* date tonight."

I dropped my hand back down to my side. The touch was so...tender. It was unnerving with everyone watching.

"I'm sure." It was only a tiny fib, and a necessary one—I hated seeing that torment on such a beautiful face.

He blew out a breath. "Okay."

"Bye for now." I kissed his cheek and backed away, wishing I were as good at winking as he was. I turned and headed toward the gymnasium entrance, and away from that bitch Shelly. Good riddance.

He called after me, "Where will you be?"

"Around." I waved at him over my head, not bothering to look back. I knew what he was looking at—I had tailored my dress to fit just so around my hips, the delicate strings of beads swinging around the tops of my thighs.

"Okay, don't go too far."

I smirked to myself as his voice faded behind me, the noise of the makeshift ballroom drowning him out. Inside, it was gloomy in the corners and twinkling with light from a rotating disco ball over the central court, the abiding smell of sweaty gym socks and leather balls seeping from adjoining locker rooms and equipment closets. Orange and white streamers clung to the corners of the wooden bleachers, which were collapsed along the walls for the party, cascading in bulk in an attempt to dress them up. I wondered how much Tristan's mother had been involved in the decorations. She just loved sprucing up the shabby.

And *someone* must have had to rush to get that photo from yesterday's game ready in time for the dance. Thanks, lady.

I wandered through the crowd, scanning it for anything helpful. I wasn't sure what. Something to occupy me for a few minutes until Tristan was done with "the first dance." Kids clustered around the edges of the basketball court, milling around folding tables with plates of food and cups of punch. They chatted explosively in groups, people packed tightly together to deliver and receive the freshest gossip.

"Like suckling piglets around mama's teats," I muttered to no one.

Unchained Melody started playing, and I wrinkled my nose in distaste. How cheesy. At least the deejay was kind of interesting, though the dance floor remained empty.

"Interesting…"

I thought of Tristan's earlier assessment that I was "the most interesting girl in school," and felt confused instead of suspicious. In hindsight, I thought he was being sincere instead of snarky, but I had no idea how he got the idea that I was interesting, or when. I had never seen him even glance in my direction at school. I usually keep to myself on campus, too, and forget about socializing after school. I supposed there were probably weekend functions and the odd party when parents were out of town, but I never showed up at that stuff. How did he even know enough about me to think about me at all?

Two girls dangerously close to my eardrums burst into excited screaming and ran into the bathroom giggling. A tangle of friends trailed behind, forcing me to stop in my tracks and halt my reflections.

You Spin Me Round, by Dead Or Alive, was pulsing out of the portable loudspeakers.

Man, the guy was really trying hard. "First, we get the oldest love song in the world for all the star-eyed couples, and now 80's British dance-pop." I remembered the latter from a Jazzercise class Cassie had made me go to once. Looked like his effort was all for naught, though; the wallflowers stood firmly planted along the outskirts, everyone waiting until someone else went first.

"And that would be Tristan and Ashley." I decided I just couldn't watch. I picked up my pace and headed for the back doors.

"Meg Shannon, I want to talk to you." Shelly appeared at my shoulder. I slowed and gazed down at her imperiously; I knew her little legs would have a hard time keeping up with mine.

"Ugh. What do *you* want?"

"I don't know what you think is going on with you and Tristan, but you should show some respect for Ashley," the venomous troll squeaked.

My lips curled over a sneer. "And why should I respect some chick I don't even know?"

"She's not just 'some chick.' She and Tristan are in love and they're meant to be together."

"I think Tristan feels a little differently…" I said, turning away from her pinched little face.

"You better not be planning to do what I think you are tonight." She grabbed my arm and yanked me back. The shrimpy thing was stronger than she looked.

"Excuse me," I glared down at her hand.

"Ashley's been waiting a long time, and they're supposed to lose that together."

"Lose *that?*" I laughed. Nice girls were so prissy, and I wanted her to say the word.

"You know what I mean, their first time," Shelly said, her face going red. "With her, not with you." Her eyes were black shiny buttons in her scrunched face. She looked me over from head to toe with distaste.

And then I was mad.

I leaned down close, to make sure she could hear, and said in a low snarl, "Get. Your. Hand. Off. Me."

She had the sense to let go of my arm.

I straightened to my full height. "Tristan has the right to do whatever he likes with his own body, in his own bedroom. And as for what I do with mine—that's none of your damn business," I said, lacing my tone with as much ice as I could summon, then stalked away.

Dead Or Alive faded out and a microphone screeched in painful feedback on stage.

"The moment we've all been waiting for, everyone…"

I winced as I finally reached the gymnasium exit and pushed through.

"I give you our newest Bobcatt King and Queen. Give it up ya'll, for Tristan Jameson and Ashley Da—"

I let the door slam behind me.

"Ugh!"

How did I get talked into coming to such a nightmare?

I leaned up against the brick wall outside, panting. I took in a slow, steadying breath, glad the night was turning cold. Crisp air filled my lungs with a cleansing tingle. The music inside rose again—was that a Justin Timberlake love song? I put my ear against the metal door and could just make out the lyrics, *"I don't wanna lose you now. I'm lookin' right at the other half of me…"*

On second thought, I hated the deejay. I pictured Tristan and Ashley spinning in a circle, her arms wrapped around his neck, adoring his Mentho-Lyptus eyes. I thought I might hurl, and I pushed myself away from the door determined to walk it off.

I hadn't gone two steps before a burst of incoherent hooting and jeering erupted from close by, then quickly died away. I stood still and listened, straining my eyes in the darkness. After a few muttered words and a moment of silence, the noise flared up again, just around the corner where light spilled around the side of the building. I crept towards it.

"Pay up, you bastard," I heard someone say once I was close enough to make out the words.

"Is that what I think it is?" I chirped, rounding the corner with glee.

When I popped my head around, half a dozen stunned faces were staring at me with eyes as wide as saucers, their owners frozen in the act of doing something illicit.

"Shit, you scared me."

"Hey, Meg."

The guys all relaxed, most of them squatting back down to haggle over bets and resume shooting dice against the sidewalk curb.

"Hey, you want in?" said my friend Chris.

He lived a few doors down from me—he was scrawny, but always sweet and often smelly. That night was no different. Apparently, not everyone shines up like a new penny. I looked around at the group, wondering what guys like that were doing at the Homecoming Dance; I counted at least two drop-outs. Well, there wasn't much better to do in Shirley, I guessed, and three counties fed into Andrew Jackson's school district.

I shook my head at Chris, "Don't have any cash." I'd spent every spare penny I had getting ready for the dance, not that I frequently had many spare pennies.

"I can spot ya," he said. "I been bleedin' these fellas dry all night."

"I couldn't pay you back, if I don't win."

"You can work it off with me, sweet tits," said a boy I didn't recognize, eyeballing those sweet body parts. He was promptly smacked in the back of the head.

"Dude!"

"Shut up, man."

I was one on the guys whenever I gambled with them, and making a remark that reminded anyone of my femaleness was strictly forbidden. The newbie blushed at his faux-pas and moved aside to let me accept a fiver from Chris.

"Alright, what are we playin', boys?" I mimed rolling up my sleeves and took my place around the pit.

A little dice would be fun, and the perfect panacea for wounded pride and blooming jealousy. I settled on my haunches and took a drag from Chris's cigarette.

"Nice flowers," he snickered.

The corsage went to my elbow and my fist went to his shoulder, hard. "Shut up."

I love street craps. It goes fast and the bets are small, so a player can stay in the game for hours with a little luck, even without winning big. As it happened, Fortuna was smiling down on me that night, and I hadn't lost once after at least half an hour. Chris's five had already turned into thirty-three, and I never mess with a winning streak. I keep betting while the dice are hot.

I was up to roll again. I had kicked off my heels and was squatting down barefoot, holding my dress closed with one hand and clicking the dice together in my other.

"Here we go—eight the hard way, y'all. Eighter from Decatur. Who's in?" I blew the dice a kiss, and it was like a fog horn in the unusual silence that had suddenly fallen.

I glanced up. The guys had gone quiet, most of them looking past me and over my head.

"What?" I said, my spine prickling already.

"Hi," said a deep voice behind me.

I knew that voice in my bones, and my skin went flush from head to toe in response. I twisted around and turned my face up towards him, smiling broadly.

"You in?" I displayed the dice in my hand and chewed my lower lip.

Several of the guys straightened up and shuffled their feet. I wondered if I should introduce my date. It wasn't exactly his crowd.

Chris stuck out his hand for Tristan to shake. "Hey, good game last night, man."

Grunts of agreement sounded all around.

Tristan kept his eyes on me. "Thanks."

I rolled the dice in my palm. Quirked an eyebrow.

"Yeah, I'm in." Tristan pulled out his wallet and threw in some cash to manly sounds of approval.

"Alright, man."

"Come on, Meg. Roll the freakin' dice already."

"No, you take 'em." I tossed the dice to one of the boys and squeezed Tristan in next to me, searching his eyes with curiosity as he crouched down on my level.

As the racket picked up around us again, he leaned close to whisper in my ear, "What are we playing?"

I chuckled softly and shook my head, "I knew it. Craps. Just follow my lead."

He paid close attention while I gave him silent clues—slight nods and smiles or the tiniest shake of my head. He kept his hand on my back and tapped out the number he thought he should bet on. I told him the right number by pressing my fingers into his thigh, if I thought he needed help. So much intimacy is involved, when teaching someone a game on the sly.

We sat so close together, I barely had to raise my voice. "How did you find me, anyway?"

"Were you hiding?" he murmured.

"No. But I'm glad you came to find me." I smiled, looking down at his sculptured lips in anticipation. When could we get out of there? "Why'd you look out here?"

"I watched you walk out, door slammer." His lips spread wide, white teeth brilliant in a teasing smile.

I felt my face turn hot and snapped my gaze back to the dice pit. He saw that, great.

"You know, Meg, you're an enigma—Yes!" He stood abruptly, and punched the sky. They all traded masculine banter over a big win.

I blinked. Enigma? What did he mean by that? Maybe I could glean more insight on my "interesting" qualities with that line of conversation. When he settled back next to me, I hoped he hadn't forgotten his last comment, because I was dying to know what he meant. But I felt too shy to ask. I settled for a questioning look. He replaced his hand on my back once more, though he was getting the hang of the game and no longer needed my instruction.

"By day you walk to classes with nerds and work in the library," he started, then wormed his fingers over to my side to tickle a rib.

"Hey! Being in advanced classes does not make you a nerd." I giggled and shoved his fingers away, hoping they'd find their way back.

They did.

"By night you gamble behind the gym in a cocktail dress."

My cheeks were aching I was smiling so hard. "Well, the cocktail dress is a rarity."

"I can't wait to see what else you can do," he said.

My heart thudded against my ribs, remembering our limo delights. His breath tickled my ear and I drank in the smell of him. A sharp tweet interrupted us, and Tristan pulled out his phone to check a text message. I read it out of the corner of my eye.

"picture time where r you? get ur ass over here!"

He grunted an expletive and dropped his face between his knees, then looked up, massaging his temples, "We gotta go in, come on."

"Now?"

"Yes, I'm sorry." He grabbed my hand to help me stand with him.

"I was on a winning streak, though."

"I'll make it up to you," he said, his smile not reaching his eyes. He ran a hand through his hair and looked towards the entrance to the gym with a frown.

Maybe it wasn't the best time to argue. I shurgged, "Alright, I guess."

I returned Chris's spot, we said bye to the guys, then headed back to the door. I shuffled through my winnings, stopping short at a bothersome thought and crumpling several bills aside. Tristan had lost all his money in the end, so I separated the wad, with about fifty bucks for each of us. "Here, take it."

"What? No." He shoved my hands away, appalled. "That's yours."

"No, it's yours."

"No."

"Come on, Tristan. I know you're cleaned out. I saw your wallet."

He shook his head resolutely and sidestepped me, "I lost, you won."

"And that's not exactly cool, since I was teaching you how to play."

I lunged forward and stuffed the money into his outside jacket pocket, cramming down his red silk handkerchief, then ran away with my hands overhead. I refused to take it back—my cost for being such a shitty instructor. It was only fair.

He caught up to me. "That's big of you, but I'll just spend it on you later." A quick, familiar kiss found my lips. A boyfriend peck.

Would there be a "later," after tonight? I was too hopeful for my own comfort and I wanted to pinch myself. I cleared my throat, "So, why were you subpoenaed?"

"Oh yeah, I forgot to tell you. They want pictures with all the Homecoming Court."

"You and Ashley," I nodded, my high spirits plummeting.

"No. No more of that, I made sure of it. They want us with our dates." He brought my hand up to his lips, then kept hold of it as he opened the door back inside. "We were subpoenaed together."

♣

He didn't let go of my hand throughout the whole argumentative photo-shoot. I was suspicious that I was being employed as a safe buffer from the venomous troll, Shelly, since she gave me a wide berth. Me and Tristan lingered on the edges of the shoot together. I held his eyes most of the time, while the other girls whined about who should stand where according to rank and height. I was surprised and pleased that no one produced the crowns, and I noticed Tristan had fallen in rank because of his loyalty to his date. The snubs were hard not to notice—a fact that sent us both into barely stifled fits of laughter and drove us further to the outskirts of the royal court ensemble.

Another couple, who seemed as disinterested in pictures as we were, drifted in our direction. Tristan introduced the guy as a junior, named John. I figured he was on the football team, too. They launched into shop talk and I looked to John's date, who seemed about as comfortable as I was. I noticed John wasn't holding her hand like Tristan was mine; she was wringing her fingers, tugging at her dress and readjusting the bodice.

I leaned over and raised my voice above the music still playing on the other side of the stage, "I'm sorry, I didn't catch your name. It's so loud in here."

"Oh. Erica. Nice to meet you."

She held out her hand, and when I tried to release Tristan's to accept the shake, he squeezed tighter. I pursed my lips and squeezed back, hard. His eyes creased at the corners when they found mine for a second. I looked pointedly at our conjoined hands, but he turned back to John and kept talking. I offered Erica an apologetic look and my left hand. She fumbled with her clutch purse as my face blazed, finally getting it under her arm and glancing at Tristan with adoration. Then at John in frustration.

"Hi," I said, pumping her hand firmly.

"Hi."

"I'm Meg. Nice to meet you, too."

She pushed imaginary glasses up on her nose, probably out of life-long habit. "That's such a cool dress. Is it a real flapper dress, like real vintage?"

"I think so." I raised my arms and scanned my figure. "It's been altered a few times, so the fit isn't really authentic."

She shook her head emphatically, "Who cares, it fits you like a glove. I love vintage stuff."

"Thank you." I couldn't remember the last time another female was so nice to me, outside of family members. "Your dress is absolutely gorgeous," I said, feeling like a gushy girlie-girl. "And you look awesome in it."

It was true. Erica's dress was a floor length, strapless satin sheath gown, and she had the body to hold it up. It looked expensive. I could tell she felt awkward in it—sort of like the ugly duckling that found her reflection in the pond and saw she was a swan, but didn't really believe it yet. I guessed this event was her first Homecoming Dance, like mine. I secreted a looked at her date, who was almost as attractive as Tristan, and I wondered what the deal was. Friends?

"Your hair looks so cool. That headband, wow."

"Oh, my cousin gave it to me." I touched my flapper version of a crown. "Yours, too. It's so elegant up like that."

Erica couldn't find the words to accept my return compliment, and merely blushed and bobbed her head instead. I shifted my weight in my high heels, wishing I had thought to clean my feet off before putting my shoes back on. They were starting to sweat, just like my hand clutched in Tristan's. I heard the music change out on the dance floor and sucked in my breath. I yanked on Tristan's hand, "Hey..."

He looked at me, his forehead furrowed in concern. "What's wrong?"

"Nothing's *wrong*. Disco!"

"Huh?"

"I have to dance to this song, Tristan. Are we done here?" I pleaded desperately.

His eyes softened. "Yeah, we're done." He signaled to one of his buddies, then let me haul him away.

"Erica, come with us," I said, waving her over to join my tiny entourage.

Erica's smile was brilliant. She grabbed John's hand, and he followed with a matching grin. I imagined myself as Cupid, loosing a golden love arrow.

"We're not done over here you guys." Shelly.

"Yeah we are," Tristan called back, jogging next to me as the four of us rounded the stage, headed for the main gym. As we all met the dance floor, he wrapped an arm around my waist and his lips met my neck, just below my ear. "You've been more than patient. Thank you."

"Screw patience. I want to dance," I yelled over the music. My fingers intertwined with his and we lunged onto the miraculously crowded basketball court.

"Good," he mouthed, letting his gaze slide over me as I started to whirl, ecstasy surely plastered on my face.

I love to dance. Rarely ever do I feel so free, so uninhibited. I let my head fall back and closed my eyes against the glittering light from the temporary disco ball, on another planet for all I cared of my surroundings. Relaxing shoulders and hips, I smiled to myself and felt my body move with the beat like it was compelled. My arms swung out around me—a trick I use to shoo away other dancers and give myself some room to move. I prefer to dance solo, since a partner just knocks me off rhythm, but boys always want to try. I sneaked a peek and saw Tristan moving around me like a satellite, blocking access and glowering at lusty-eyed rivals.

"That's sweet," I said, but the music was too loud for him to hear me. He didn't see me either, on patrol as he was.

I'd never felt so unencumbered on a dance floor and I wanted to thank him. I moved around to face him, caught his eye, and beamed him my gratitude before spinning away. The music changed and I spread my arms wide, my torso undulating with the natural current of the song, the electricity of the dance mix racing across the surface of my skin like a blue flame over spilled kerosene. Tristan caught my fingers in mid-swing and whipped me around to face him. I remembered where I had seen that blue flame before. In his eyes.

I could feel the urgency in his grip—he wanted to play, too.

"Yay!" I shot both hands in the air, gleeful.

He held onto my waist with a quizzical expression.

"Time to dance you, pretty boy," I sang, accepting his embrace.

Guys are shit dancers, for the most part. Usually when they say, "Wanna dance?" what they mean is, "Wanna grind?" But, if a boy is limber enough and we have the right points of bodily contact, I can usually get him at least moving to the same beat with me. I call it "dancing the boys." Tristan had been an excellent date so far, and I certainly didn't mind multiple points of bodily contact with him.

I locked my shape with his; hands, shoulders, hips, and thighs. But he wasn't used to being physically overpowered. He reeled me in and held the small of my back with authority, his fingers stretched wide enough to wrap around the sides of my waist and move me where he wanted me. I twisted my arms around his neck and held on. He was dancing *me*. With my four-inch heals, we were almost the same height, and his lips were less than an inch away from mine. As a slow song began to drift into my ears, I felt my hips roll easily with his.

Whoa. He was actually a good dancer. "Years of athletic training must help you to gracefully react against opposing force," I thought out loud. That was stupid. How did he rattle my mind so fast?

"Huh?"

"Just. You know, most guys don't. I don't know..."

"What are you talking about?" He leaned in so close I could feel his breath on my ear. "Just dance with me."

I nodded, incapable of speech. Yes. Just dance.

We pressed together in gentle friction and I forgot place and time. How did I finally find someone I could move so perfectly with? It was like we'd taken dancing lessons together for years. Erotic dancing lessons. I felt him stiffen against my pelvis and I pushed into it, grabbing his hips. Not even hearing the song anymore, my body took on a more carnal rhythm of its own.

"Meg," Tristan said, his voice rumbling deep within his chest, vibrating against mine. "Let's get outta here."

I nodded eagerly and let him lead me off the dance floor. I barely registered faces flashing in the strobe light, bodies ebbing and flowing past me in more casual celebration. Tristan shoved through the outer doors. My face was so flushed that the cold air felt like a slap on my cheeks. But, I've never really listened to warnings like that.

chapter six

He let Barney open the door without complaint, supporting me and patiently stalling my groping hands until we were in the privacy of the cabin. Before I heard the click of the door lock, we tumbled onto the floor in a tangle of limbs. My crazy afro of ringlets was everywhere, but I didn't care. I plunged my hands between us, my fingers fumbling desperately for buttons and zippers, but Tristan took them in a firm grip.

"Wait," he said in a ragged voice. He sat up. "Just wait."

Blowing out a long, slow breath, he closed his eyes and brought outstretched hands towards his lap, palms down in a calming gesture. I rose from the floor and propped myself on my elbow, confused. He just sat there breathing, lips pursed, while I watched him, barely daring to breathe.

Finally, he opened his eyes and smiled. "Okay."

The limo started rolling and I grasped the carpet to avoid toppling over. The sound of my own throat clearing crackled through the cabin. We pulled out of the school parking lot and turned onto the state road, and Tristan turned to watch the countryside flow past outside through the panoramic window. What the hell did I do? I thought "the benefits" were the reason he asked me to the damn dance in the first place. I clenched my fists in the carpet to stop myself from throwing them in the air, then I put them in my lap, feigning demure. Demure my ass. I wanted to attack him and he was done with me, apparently.

He smiled down at my hands twisted together, pried them apart, and pulled me up to sit with him on the seat. A shoulder squeeze and a forehead kiss, then he reached over to switch on the radio. I looked out the window on my side, hoping to hide the horror on my face.

What the hell just happened? What changed his mind? I closed my eyes and let my thoughts race, trying to recall the last few minutes where things must have gone wrong. Everything seemed to be going okay before we started dancing together, then…I sort of lost control. Our exodus was abrupt. He said he liked me wild, but maybe that was too wild. I pictured the scene, imagining how I must've looked, clinging to him like a stripper on a dancer's pole. Dancing always makes me lose myself. I blinked at the streetlights zooming past, wondering who he saw watching us dance that had embarrassed him so much.

"I'm sorry I got carried away back there," I whispered, miserable.

"Are you kidding? I was the one having to count to ten."

My head snapped around. "What?"

"I'm glad you can't read my thoughts," he said, raising his eyebrows and chuckling quietly. "They might've scared you."

"I doubt it."

"Trust me," he snorted. "Girls never know the half of what guys are thinking."

I gaped at him. He shook his head and looked back outside at the passing landscape.

"I don't get it," I said, finally alert enough to my surroundings to recognize where we were. We were driving northwards into the valley, not south to the mountain cove where I lived. "Wait. Aren't you taking me home?"

"Do you want me to?"

"No. I just thought…where are we going?"

"To my house. Didn't I tell you? I thought everyone knew my mom and dad went out of town this weekend, to leave the place to me and Amanda. Sorry, I should have asked if that was cool with you."

"So, you're having a party or something?"

He shook his head like he was dislodging an uncomfortable memory. "No. That's why everyone's so pissed off at me. Or, one of the reasons. I don't know, I think my sister's having a couple friends spend the night. They're just sophomores, though. They won't bother us."

"Oh."

Ooooh…

"Should I tell Barney to turn around—"

"No!" I grabbed his arm before I could stop myself. Seconds before, I was dreading the night I thought lay ahead of me: lying alone in my bed all night, sleep impossible. I would've sorted through every detail of my fantasy date with Tristan, over and over, sifting for clues as to what had gone wrong. I may have murdered Piper in her sleep, to silence her habitual, incessant snoring in the next room. "I mean, are you asking me to spend the night with you?"

"Well, yeah. Is that wrong to ask?"

I looked at him in the dark cabin, the music flowing around us drifting into my consciousness. Our classical station was playing Pachelbel's *Canon in D*, the famous, ultra-romantic string composition so popular at weddings. It was an odd moment. What could've been considered a lewd invitation—a crude assumption—was made sweet and romantic. Tristan's shy smile helped.

"No, it's not wrong. I'd love to. Thank you."

"Good." He leaned over with a lingering kiss, then settled back onto the seat beside me. "I'd love to have you."

Butterflies again. I couldn't remember the last guy who had riled up those tiny rainbow-winged beasts so much. I tried to relax and sort my thoughts, watching the valley roll past. The fact was, falling for a guy like Tristan Jameson was the dumbest thing a girl like me could do. I preferred not to feel anything for guys—it was the only way to avoid being hurt by them—and Tristan was in a totally different social strata than my own. I wanted to have fun that night, but I just had to keep my head together and not let my heart take over. That's what I tried to tell myself. But it felt too good to have him look at me like that, with those, blue, blue eyes.

Before long, a walled subdivision came into view. Tristan pressed a button, and the window dividing us from Barney slid down. "Heard anything from my sister yet?"

"Not a word since I dropped her and her friends at the high school after you."

"Nice. I hope she stays at the dance for a while. My mom made us split the limo tonight," Tristan explained in an aside to me. "You're a bargain, right Barney? Driving all over the valley for Jameson & Co."

Barney lifted a shoulder, "Ain't been no trouble."

"I'm sure you know where to go, after two trips there already."

"Yes, sir. No problem."

Sir. I smiled at Tristan and he returned a goofy grin. We left the window open while Barney drove through the twisting streets, lined with old-fashioned iron street lamps, scattered picket fences, and low hedges. We pulled up in the Jameson driveway and as the car rolled to a stop, Tristan reached through the window clapped Barney on the shoulder, with a crisp bill between two fingers. "Been a pleasure."

So, there was a secret pocket in that wallet. Sneaky.

"Aw, Mrs. Jameson took care of that already, sir."

"That's extra. So you might drive extra slow on the way home with my sister. And so you'll let me open the door for my own date?"

Barney laughed. "I'll take your sister for ice cream, how's that?"

"Perfect." Tristan shook his hand before sliding off the seat and opening our door. He waited in the street for me, his hair fallen over his eyes and his smile mischievous. I scooted towards the exit, retrieving my heels and slipping them on before accepting his help out.

I looked back at the limo as we walked up the driveway. "Is he just gonna to sit there?"

Barney had moved out to the street and was clearly parked for the duration. He turned off the engine and cranked his seat back, the blue glow of a miniature flat screen display already lighting up his face and the sound of a sports announcer floating out of his cracked window.

"Until Amanda needs him to pick her up, probably. The limo company is based in Tenakho Falls, over an hour from here."

"Kinda nice to have a massive bodyguard stationed outside your house."

"I guess." Tristan shrugged as he pulled a lanyard of keys from under his shirt.

I felt a warm whoosh of air when he pulled the door open, and the smell of cinnamon and fresh bread swept over me. Someone had been baking recently. A lot. "You're sure no one is here? What if they decided to come back early?"

His mother was so present with those happy homemaker smells, that it was hard to believe she wasn't sitting in the dark somewhere, waiting to catch us. I felt naughty.

"Don't worry, they're making a weekend of it. They won't be back until tomorrow night. Late."

I stepped inside the foyer, still a little unsure, and looked around in the dimness. I've never been comfortable meeting parents and generally feel unwelcome in boys' homes, especially with their mothers around. The place did seem empty, though—silent, except for the slow tick-tock of a grandfather clock directly across from the front door.

"So...this is it," said Tristan, a little too loudly.

The peculiar note in his voice snapped me out of my timidity, and I turned to him in wonder. "So it is."

He was fidgeting with his keys and rocking from his heels to the balls of his feet, all wooden and shy.

Aw. He was nervous. How cute. "And now what?" I felt compelled to ask.

"Are you hungry or thirsty? You want something to eat?" He motioned towards the kitchen, then scratched the back of his neck. "Like a sandwich or something. I think there's cake—my mom made one for the Pumpkin Festival this weekend and one for us to keep. It's pretty good."

"I'm hungry alright. Not for food."

He blushed and I caught my breath; Tristan Jameson just got hotter. I glanced past the kitchen, where I had no intention of going, and into a long, dark hallway. Where was his room? I was starting to worry that he might chicken out, and I thought we better get this after-party started before he did. How could I move things in a better direction than his mother's cake?

I reached out and ran my finger along the bottom edge of his tuxedo vest. "How long are you gonna make me wait, you big tease?"

He let out the breath that he had been holding and flashed me a smile that made my knees weak. "Yeah, pretty long night."

He was still rooted to the welcome mat.

"Give me a tour?" I offered.

"Sure." He took my hand; it was sweaty, but at least he was touching me and not jingling his keys from hand to hand anymore. We both knew neither of us had any intention of touring, but I was surprised when he led me away from the long hallway and towards another wing of the house. I stopped short when we ended up in front of a door to what was obviously the master bedroom.

"Your parents' room?"

"My sister's room is right next to mine. I don't want her bothering us." He rolled his eyes, then added, "Plus, my room isn't nice enough." He turned the handle and pushed the door open.

I frowned, unsure. But the idea of deflowering the quarterback in his mother's bed gave me a perverse thrill, especially since I had been expressly forbidden to do so. I followed him inside with a private smirk.

The room was huge—almost like a separate suite all to itself, with a seating area around a TV and a door that opened onto a private bathroom. Someone had left a light on by the commode, and I could tell the bathroom was bigger than my living room. The bedroom itself was dimly lit by a small table lamp next to the bed. And when my eyes roamed past the lamp...

"Oh my god."

The bed was covered in rose petals. I swiveled on my heels to gape at him, then at the bed, speechless.

"Do you like roses? My mom has about a million of them in our back-yard. I didn't think she'd notice if a few were stolen."

"A few? Looks more like a few dozen." The entire king size bed was covered with them—red, pink, white, yellow.

"It's October. They needed pruning anyway."

"Just part of your yard work chores?"

"No," he said softly.

I was being rude, I realized, and I felt like a jerk. "They're beautiful. I love roses." Actually, I wasn't too familiar with them before that night.

While he searched a night stand drawer under the lamp, I noticed the candles. Lighter in hand, Tristan moved around the room, igniting each one, until the whole suite was aglow in warm, dancing, incandescent light. It was magical.

"Ouch." My fingernails bit into the flesh at the back of my own arm. He turned and smiled at me, and went to put the lighter away.

I didn't understand. Why all the effort? All the wining and dining and romance. It really wasn't necessary, and I almost said so. But, he was approaching me with a crooked smile. An innocent smile. Then everything made sense. The limo, the champagne, his sister wanting to help, the bed full of roses, him not letting things go too far in the car on the way to his house. That stupid twit Shelly's infuriating demands.

All this wasn't for me, it was for him. This was a special night for him and he'd been waiting a long time, too. How many times had Ashley turned him down? No matter how gorgeous he was, being rejected hurt. Prolonged, constant rejection by someone who supposedly loved you must have been unbearable. Years as the acting mother for all my younger siblings had honed my nurturing urges, and I felt like cradling Tristan's head against my chest, stroking his face like I would with Charlie when he'd had a nightmare or skinned a knee.

That wasn't going to help, though.

My heart ached for him. He looked so unsure. If he'd had pockets in his tuxedo pants, he probably would've stuffed his hands deep inside them. I looked around the room, searching for something, but I wasn't sure what. There was a glimmer in the darkness outside, just past the sliding glass doors. The view was partially blocked by vertical blinds, but I caught the unmistakable flash of a slice of moon reflected in water. "Is that a swimming pool out there?"

"Oh yeah," he said, brightening. He reached past me and flicked a switch on the wall. The pool materialized in blue-green brilliance. "Want to swim?"

"It's probably too cold, isn't it?"

"It's heated. My dad keeps it open until November usually—after Halloween, when the jack-o'-lanterns have all rotted. That's his signal to close it up for the winter. We'll probably carve Pumpkins next week, actually. It know it's weird but we still have a jack-o-lantern contest, even though my youngest sister is already in high school. Very fierce family competition. The pool's salt water, too, so we won't reek of chlorine after we swim."

Nervous rambling again. I had to act fast. "I'd love to swim."

"Okay, cool. I'll go get us some towels."

I watched him leave.

Since I didn't have a suit, skinny-dipping was obvious, and I have never known a guy to resist for long after seeing me naked. No more over-thinking. I eased off my flapper headband, laid it on the bureau, and grabbed a pencil I saw there. My zipper went down and my straps went to the brink of my shoulders. Facing the glass doors, I made sure they were unlocked, and when I heard Tristan's footsteps returning, I let the heavy beaded thing drop straight down to my ankles. I sighed in relief. Then I stepped out, one foot at a time, bending over slowly to remove first one shoe, then the next. Satin panties dropped and I kicked them aside. Without turning to acknowledge Tristan, I eased open the sliding door and stepped outside.

Shit, it was cold. But, I strolled around the edge of the pool until I was facing him on the other side, pretending to ignore his presence. Goose bumps were rising on my arms, but I took my time twisting my hair up and fixing it with the pencil. I stepped into the warm water and tiptoed down the steps. Once I was submerged up to my waist, I looked up to see Tristan slipping outside, already naked himself. He closed the door behind him and set the towels on a lawn chair in a hurry, not bothering to pretend he wasn't. The beauty of his body was astonishing, the glow from the pool illuminating every curve from below as he strode across the patio. He was a present unwrapped. All night I had wanted to get him out of that tuxedo—to see that long, lean, muscular body, built for the speed and precision he was known for on the field. But in the flesh, it was almost too much. Every inch of him was perfection, as if chiseled into marble. He slid into the water like a demigod from a Greek poem.

Suddenly I was the one feeling like a fumbling, awkward virgin—until our bodies found each other in the fevered heat of the pool. Within minutes, we were racing across the patio back to the bedroom, laughing and shivering, hastily drying off before plunging under the down comforter. Rose petals flew in the air.

"My roses," I gasped, almost serious.

He pushed the petals away, his voice rasping, "I'll get you some more."

What happened to my shy schoolboy? He had vanished, replaced by tender lips and sure hands. Soft kisses followed my clavicle and made their way down my chest. He traced the line of my waist with his fingertips and sent goose bumps prickling up to my breasts. Then he kissed those, too. His skin was already warmed, his whole body radiating heat, the weight of him delicious as I clung to him.

Gentle and demanding at once, it was like he had a map of my body and my mind. "How do you know exactly how to touch me?"

He smoothed my hair back from my face and nudged my nose with his. "I've been thinking about this for a long time."

It was all so overwhelming I was panting. "With me?"

"With you."

I threaded my fingers into his hair and shook my head, confused. "I don't understand."

"You're so different from everyone else." He brushed his lips over my mouth, my cheeks, and I closed my eyes. "You don't hide who you are." He kissed my eyelids, one by one. "So beautiful. Deep down." A warm hand rested on my chest, over my heart. "I can see the real you."

The real me. The real me. I breathed him in all around me and hugged his chest to mine.

"I want to know you, Meg. Every inch of you." It was barely a whisper.

He gathered my hair behind my neck and twisted my face to his, insistent and almost desperate, his lips suddenly hard and his hands rough. I felt my knee pressed into my shoulder, his erection hot against my thigh. In a daze, I heard him digging in the night stand, a condom in place so fast I barely registered what he was doing until it was done. I was shocked and thrilled and I could hardly get my words out right, "I want to know you. Tristan, I do."

chapter seven

I watched him sleeping.

Sigh.

I almost said it out loud, I felt so foolish: "Great job, Meg. Just go ahead and sleep with him right away, just like everyone said you would. Don't leave anything to the imagination, just let him have it all."

I rolled over onto my back, angry at my own trepidation bubbling up inside my gut.

"Stop it, you dork," I admonished myself silently. I don't need to fall in love with someone in order to have sex, and I never have. Rules like that were for brainwashed lemmings who would follow the crowd off a cliff rather than think an original thought.

Plus, love is even more dangerous than sex.

I let my head loll to the side for another look at Sleeping Beauty. He was so peaceful. I had never seen anyone look so gorgeously relaxed, in deep, blissful slumber. His lips were slightly parted, irises darting under their lids in a dream state. The lines of tension in his forehead I had noticed off and on all night were completely smoothed away.

Yes, he was a delicious sight. But it wasn't love.

I flounced onto my back and watched the ceiling for a few minutes.

And damn it, I didn't want it to be love. Right?

I scowled at his adorable, cupid's bow mouth. There was no way I could keep still enough not to disturb him, so I eased out from under the covers, trying to feel annoyed at his sleeping face rather than enamored. How could he just pass out like that? Sure, he said some nice things—guys would say anything to reach the holy grail—but he was gone as soon as he got what he wanted. I myself was still zinging head to toe, nowhere near sleep.

And starving.

I wandered the room, focused on procuring food instead of the tightness in my chest. Errant doubts invaded my head, relentless. I had to concentrate on eating, not the amazing male specimen lying naked in bed. Although the thought of that pumpkin cake he mentioned earlier set my stomach growling instantly, I didn't want to go into the kitchen without him in case his sister came home to find a stranger rummaging through the fridge. My mind finally settled on the image of a miniature cheesecake at the bottom of the picnic bag. I had to have it. It would still be in the limo; we'd been too distracted when we got out, and I didn't remember grabbing that bag or my purse. I remembered focusing on Tristan's eyes.

"Brilliant, Meg. Just brilliant," said that naggy little voice.

Hoping Barney was still waiting in the car, I found my dress puddled by the sliding glass door and slipped it on as quietly as I could. I looked back at Tristan, still dead to the world. It was probably safer to go out through the front, since the cold air from the patio might wake up my suddenly inattentive date. Shivering, I plucked Tristan's tuxedo jacket off the floor, then padded out of the master bedroom barefooted. I slunk down the hallway and peeked through the leaded glass window by the front door.

The limo was still parked outside. "Yes!"

Barney let me into the main cab to grab the cheesecake and my purse, then begrudgingly obliged as I climbed into the front to listen to the comedy channel with him. I didn't give him much choice. We munched cheesecake together, him chuckling intermittently at some comedian I'd never heard of and me winding myself up into a frenzy of second-guessing.

Would Tristan even talk to me at school on Monday? He never talked to me before...

God, why did I go all the way?

Wait. I don't say things like, "go all the way."

I slapped my knee in irritation, provoking a curious look from Barney. I grinned and he shook his head, then looked away.

"Go all the way" sounded as archaic as "heavy petting." That kind of thinking was not what I was about. I had sex with him because I wanted to have sex with him, damn it.

Barney's laugh turned into a roar at some joke the comedian cracked; his broad shoulders shook and tears streamed from the corners of his eyes. I couldn't help but join in, even though I had no idea what had just been said.

I felt better after the endorphin rush. Tristan really did seem to like me, too. I remembered him holding my hand during the photo shoot, and the look in his eyes when he said I was beautiful, deep down. I chewed on a strand of my hair. Maybe he really did mean the stuff he said. I flicked a cheesecake crumb off my knee. Would it be that strange, the two of us together?

A look out the window, in the direction of the master bedroom, reminded me how far apart our worlds were. Such a beautiful house.

"It *would* be strange. It was one date, Meg," I had to remind myself privately. "Don't lose your head."

I thought of him inside, dreaming, with rose petals all around him. Those were the first roses a guy had ever given me—no, the second. The second in one night, counting the corsage.

"Fine. I'm just gonna roll with it," I said aloud.

"Pardon me?" Barney's pitch ticked up in surprise.

Yes, I *did* want to cuddle up with Tristan again in those roses. But not yet. I wanted to do something crazy first, something that didn't involve falling for the freaking quarterback. I had to reclaim myself, before all was lost. The clock on the dashboard said it was almost midnight. Was it possible to still get in a hand or two?

"Barney, do you play poker?"

He frowned at me, suspicious. "On occasion...sure."

"Want to take me to a game, not too far from here? You know where After Dark is? It's a little entertainment spot in the hills."

"A bar?" He looked me over, not bothering to hide his disapproval.

"Now Barney, this is a dry county. No alcohol allowed," I said, with what I hoped was a seductive smile.

"You're outta your mind, girl." He shook his head and looked out the driver-side window.

"Come on, it's almost midnight. I know you're off the clock soon."

"So?"

"What do I have to do to get you to take me? Come on."

"Show me your tits," he snorted. I reached to pull the straps of my dress over my shoulders. "That was a joke—pull those back up!" His pitch hit the roof and he looked around wildly to make sure no one had seen. "What's wrong with you?"

"If you don't take me, I'll just have to walk." I gathered up the cheesecake trash and made to get out of the car.

He started up the engine and glared at me sideways, "Alright, Jesus."

"Whatever happened to Amanda anyway?" I settled into my seat happily, making conversation.

"I have no idea," he muttered, then looked at me out of the corner of his eye again. I detected a smile. "I'm off the clock remember. Ain't no baby-sitter."

"Ain't indeed." I rubbed my hands together; that fifty bucks would get me in, and I knew I could run it up. In a much better mood, I found a good rock station and cranked it up. "I love this song." I cheered and sang along as Barney drove out of the valley and up into the trashier parts of Shirley County.

♥

Barney decided to accompany me inside once we arrived, though he said he couldn't get involved in a poker game. I could tell he was nervous to simply drop me off when he got a good look at After Dark, and as it turned out, I was glad to be on his arm as we walked in. More than one set of bloodshot eyes fixed first on my dress, then on my chest, then on my bare feet. When the gazes finally roamed to the hugely muscled man towering over me, each guy quickly found some-thing more wholesome—pool cue, television, or empty tumbler—to occupy his attention. I usually came to the place in jeans and a T-shirt, and looking down at my beaded dress, I saw how shortsighted I had been not to have thought of that. I pulled Tristan's tuxedo jacket closed, buttoning myself in as best as I could. It hung on me like a sack, a protective barrier.

"Meg! What are you doing here?"

I turned to the familiar voice in relief. Larry. He used to date my mom back in the day and was sort of an uncle figure to me and my siblings. "Hi, Larry. Not too late for me to get in a hand or two, is it?"

"Nah, come on back. Love to have you, sweet thang," he said, motion-ing to the bartender with authority.

Barney lifted an eyebrow in question and I nodded. "Thanks for the ride, I've got friends in the back." I extended my arms as far as they would go to give him a hug around his wide shoulders. "See you around," I said, knowing I'd likely never see him again.

"I'll stay for a while," he said loudly, offering the look of a bouncer all around. He claimed a bar stool and folded his arms across his chest.

"Thanks," I smiled, touched. In a way, Barney had been a big part of my magical night. I made my way to the back, hoping that magic was still in effect.

Cards are one of my favorite pastimes, especially poker. But I rarely had enough cash to play at After Dark, even though I was finally old enough to play there. The buy-in was fifty dollars, usually too steep for me. That night, if I borrowed a little from Tristan, I'd have enough to hang for a while.

"Thanks, Tristan. You don't mind, do you?" I said, patting the front pocket of his jacket. I knew he wouldn't, and I'd split the winnings with him to make up for it. If I didn't win…well, he said he would only spend it on me later anyway. He was buying me a good time, even passed out as he was. It was his fault I had to have fun without him, and I felt luckier with his involvement by monetary contribution. It was weird, but I had been feeling a lucky streak all that day. Things had just fallen into place, and the feeling only intensified when Tristan came to pick me up. The Tristan Effect. I mused over my new lucky charm as I walked into the card room, and—one more fortunate detail—my cousin Zach was there, with an empty seat next to him.

I rounded the table practically skipping. "Zach, did you finally get some big boy pants?"

"You should talk." He squeezed me in a bear hug. Already tight enough to be painful, he constricted my chest further to force a squeak from my lungs, like I was a baby toy. He loves to do that. We're less than two months apart in age, and I had towered over him for most of our childhood. It was only in the past three years that I stopped getting taller and Zach hit a colossal growth spurt. Plenty of time in a weight room helped to enhance the effect. He rubbed it in and abused his strength whenever possible.

"You'll pay for that, junior," I said as he set me down. Since I was technically his superior in age, I never let him forget it.

"Can't wait to see you try, kitten." Of course, he would always have the upper hand at poker tables in Shirley County, him being a guy and Shirley being totally sexist. I scowled at him and he chuckled, "I win."

"For now." He had no idea how my day was going, But, I thought it wise to keep my secret Tristan Jameson weapon private.

I placed my money on the table, already nicely broken up from dice wagering. Those guys rarely used chips, and it pissed them off if you didn't bring enough for change. I nodded to the other fellas, some of whom I knew pretty well, before sitting down next to my cousin. I smiled at Ricky; he was in me and Zach's class at Andrew Jackson, and one of my best friends. Well, one of my only friends. Terry Finley was a guy who lived in my neighborhood—kind of a scumbag. One of the old cowboys I'd seen at Coleman Ranch had stiffened when I pulled out my chair, but Sean McBride gave him a thumbs up in my honor, and the man nodded curtly. Sean was my first boyfriend when I was in middle school. He had been a senior in high school at the time, and he could've gotten in a lot of trouble messing around with someone so young. But I've kept my mouth shut to this day, and he damn well better give me the A-okay.

"Hey, Ricky. Hey, Sean," I said. Terry Finley squinted across the table. Did he expect a hello, too, gross old lech? I always thought he looked like a wife beater.

I recognized another face and smiled as its owner tipped his baseball hat to me and started to stand, but stopped himself, embarrassed. Mal was so old-fashioned. Everyone knew him and liked him. He had been the mail carrier for the southern half of Shirley County for decades, almost a permanent fixture in the neighborhood. He had even consented to play penny cards with me and my friends once or twice on this or that doorstop, and he'd revealed many poker secrets to our hungry young ears.

"What are we playing?" I asked, trying to sound as nonchalant as possible, though I was nervous as shit. Real poker at After Dark, here we go.

"Seven-Card Stud," said Zach.

I plastered on my poker face. My favorite—could this night get any better? "Hi-lo?"

"High."

"Wild cards?"

"Nope."

"Pot limit?"

Ricky broke in, "Of course not. Shit, Meg. Why don't you get here on time next game?"

"Just trying to get my bearings, keep your shirt on." I knew anytime I arrived was fine with Ricky. He'd had a crush on me since elementary school. "I had to be somewhere," I said, motioning to my strange costume of red dress, tent-like tuxedo jacket, and bare feet. "Why didn't *you* go?"

"Cuz you never came to pick me up. I was waitin' all night," said Ricky.

Sean cleared his throat.

"Please," agreed an older gentleman I didn't recognize. He looked like a banker from out of town.

That was as far as romantic allusion went at the card table. I glared at Ricky, willing him to be quiet and not ruin my cool. He grinned and goosed my knee under the table. I jerked away, but couldn't stop a tiny giggle from escaping. Infuriating.

"So, speaking of time..." said the banker, pointing to his wrist.

"Just waitin' on Larry."

"Yo, Larry!"

"I gotta take a piss, then."

"Come on, man."

Jesus, like a bunch of old ladies. I was feeling much more confident listening to them all bicker and whine. It's funny how reality is never as good as the imagination. Well, almost never. I pushed a memory of Tristan's perfect, chiseled abdomen out of my mind. I had to concentrate, and not on that.

Larry came back with a lidded tray that he put by his feet. A few seconds later, a shot of whiskey appeared by my elbow. So the secret shooter tradition was true. It was one of the things Zach, Ricky, and I had found so fascinating about the famed, illicit After Hours poker game as adolescents. I knocked it back in one gulp, keeping my face as neutral as I could—but god was it nasty—and sat it upside down on the floor. Everyone else did the same, the ritual so firmly established as to be practically law.

"Youngest scrounges," reminded Larry.

"Oh, Zachary angel. I think that's you," said Ricky.

I tried not to smile but Zach saw it anyway and flipped me off.

But law was law, and Zach got down under the table, retrieved everyone's glasses, and snapped the top back over the tray. Larry slid it towards the door with his foot. Even there, the Shirley County prohibition on alcohol loomed large, and no one would risk a night in the sheriff's drunk tank by being sloppy.

The sheriff...

Sheriff Jameson—that was Tristan's dad. Heat rose in my cheeks and it had nothing to do with the whiskey. I thought of what awaited me, naked and sleeping in the sheriff's own bed, and I was antsy to get the game started.

"And without further ado..." Larry, the unofficial leader of the poker club, finally called, "Ante up, boys. Five buckaroos."

I resisted the urge to rub my hands together and let out an evil chortle. Eat your heart out Ashley Freakin' Davis. She was probably decked out in hoodie-footie pajamas at a slumber party with that bitch Shelly. Old Maid or Go Fish?

Everyone threw in but Ricky, who was still underage, poor lamb. Larry was adamant about the age restriction—absolutely no players under eighteen. He hadn't been in on the shots, either. Larry upheld his own laws faithfully. He shuffled, let the cowboy split the deck, then shuffled again. He burned the first card, then slid each player their first hole card in turn. I noticed that no one else peeked at that one, so I waited, too. One more down, then one card facing up. My heart fell when I saw mine: two of hearts. I glanced around the table. A couple more low cards were scattered around, but Sean had the ace of diamonds and the banker had the king of spades.

Damn it.

Ricky sent me silent sympathy with his eyes and patted my thigh under the table. I pinched the top of his hand as hard as I could, nails extended.

I finally reached for my hole cards to have a look. Another two, that one in diamonds. Things were looking up. At least I had a pair, though a low one. I turned up a corner of my second blind: the seven of spades. Well.

I knew it was cheesy to feel a tremor of excitement run through me, because everyone's lucky number is seven. And I'm not a superstitious person, except when it comes to cards. Two of hearts may not have seemed fortuitous at first, but there with the lucky seven of spades? Spades represented the sword of a knight, and what was my Tristan if not some strange high school Homecoming knight in shining armor?

"Meg, you got the low card. What are you waitin' for?"

"Oh, sorry. What's the bring-in?"

"Twenty," the wife beater snapped in irritation. I could almost hear him thinking "dumb bitch" underneath.

All the better. I decided to play the bimbo role—my personal riff on the poker face. Zach would know what I was doing, but he had a low card showing, too, and he sighed when he looked at his blinds.

"Okay. I guess I'm in?" I tossed in my money.

Larry, who was to my left and next in the betting round, gave me a fatherly look as if to say, "You sure, sweet thang?"

I ignored him.

"Alright…call that," he said with a shrug and shoved a twenty toward the pile.

"Call," said the wife beater.

"Fold," said Mal, and handed Larry his cards. I saw that he had at least one spade, as Larry flipped them over next to his arm.

The banker was next. He had a five card showing. Another spade. "I fold."

Wimps. Come on, let's run this up some more.

The rancher tossed in a twenty and made a hand gesture. I took mental notes.

Sean nodded and added his money to the pot.

I could tell Zach was unsure, but then he pulled a couple bills from his wad, too. "Yeah, call."

Larry passed around our next card, face-up.

Mine was a seven of clubs, to my delight. Two pair then. With the way my night was going, I wasn't afraid to hope for a full house. I smiled inside and snuggled into Tristan's jacket, his cologne wafting up, spicy and warm. I heard Ricky chuckle beside me (my hand showing didn't look promising), and I punched him on the shoulder, making sure to display an embarrassed pout while I cased my competition.

Larry handed Sean another ace.

Crap.

He flipped over another jack for himself—that was a pair of jacks for him.

Double crap.

Sean had the high hand showing, so it was his choice to check or bet. I knew Sean pretty well and he was notoriously macho. I knew he'd keep it rolling. He grunted something incomprehensible and threw in another twenty dollar bill.

Zach's eyes darted around to the other players, his fingers thrumming the table. "Fuck." He crammed his cards together and handed them to Larry.

I was next.

I was sweating. After I made a move, they'd know I had something. It was all in or all out. I didn't want anyone to fold too fast, though—the pot wasn't heavy enough. "I'll raise your bet, Mr. McBride," I said, trying to sound dumb and chipper as I tossed in a twenty and a ten. I saw Zach narrow his eyes. He was onto me, but he was already out of the game. Ricky elbowed him under his arm and grinned at me. Stop it, Ricky, you ass.

Larry shrugged and met my raise; he had tons of money and he liked to keep the game running.

The wife beater folded in disgust and I felt the chill in his gaze down to my toes.

The cowboy had gained the four of spades to go with his king. He met the raise without hesitation.

Shit, was he working on a flush? That would totally beat what I had so far.

Sean threw in another ten for my raise, then Larry looked to each of us in silent question. The bet went around the table again and everyone simply stayed, then we were ready for our fifth card, face up.

"Alright, y'all," said Larry, as he flipped over another spade right in front of the cowboy.

Oh no.

The cowboy had three spades showing, but he needed five for a flush. What were his blind cards? My mind raced, trying to remember how many spades I had already seen that game.

Damn that whiskey.

Sean smiled and pulled a third ace next to his other two.

Then, I almost lost it when I saw Larry flipped over a seven of hearts in front of me. I had a full house! That beat everything showing around the table. Hallelujah and thank you, my sweet good luck charm. In my mind, I nuzzled Tristan's sleepy face with my cheek. He'd be so warm and cozy right about then.

But, Sean still had the high hand showing, with three aces. He threw in forty bucks and smirked at me. A big raise. He knew my game by then, and he was trying to intimidate me. Four of a kind would beat my full house, but there was no way he had another ace in his blind. The odds were like four-thousand to one. I looked at the cowboy. He could be going for a flush—I doubted it, with all those spades I'd seen flying—but now that I had a full house, he didn't stand a chance anyway.

I added up all my bets. I would be gratuitously dipping into Tristan's cash.

If I stalled more than a few seconds, I was done.

The cowboy fiddled with his hands, and I knew he was waiting for the game to pass to him so he could fold. Larry had nothing, the game was over for him; he glanced towards the door, probably wondering how long he'd have to wait before heading back to the bar. I fingered the bills in my pocket. Tristan's pocket. The decision was made.

"I'll see your raise," I added forty bucks to the pot. "And raise another twenty." My skin felt singed when I let go of those last bills.

"I'm done," said Larry, scooping his cards together and marrying them to the discard.

The cowboy's face contorted like he was constipated. "Fold," he finally produced.

Sean held my gaze and nodded to Larry.

One more card up.

Nothing on either side.

"Check," said Sean.

"Check," I agreed, relieved. At least I wouldn't have to add more money to stay in. I was out of cash. Maybe Sean was, too.

The last card was blind. I hardly dared to peek. I stared at Sean hard, until he finally broke away to look under his last card. He was faltering—he couldn't beat me and he knew it. But he was such an asshole. He still had the highest hand showing, so the bet went to him. If he decided to bet or raise, I couldn't meet it. I was cleaned out.

Damn it, I was so close! What was I gonna say to Tristan, if I lost it all?

A lit cigarette butt sailed into the room through the open doorway, and landed on the card table.

chapter eight

"Hey!" Larry was on his feet with an immediate violent reaction, like most of the guys. "What do you think this is, your goddamn toilet?"

"Sombitch…" was the garbled expletive, just outside the door—some drunk fool probably on his way to the bathroom, tossing his finished smoke before stumbling past to take a piss. A split second later, a glass mug exploded on the door next to Larry's head.

"You gone be sorry for that, you piece-a-trash." The cowboy had the thick end of half a pool cue in his fist and he was already across the room, holding it cocked back like a baseball bat over his shoulder.

Sean said, "Show me," rolling up his sleeves, his glare focused past me.

I flipped my cards over and he glanced at the table.

"Nice hand. Take it before somebody else does." He jerked his head towards the pile of money and bustled past me into the billiard hall. Sean was a jerk, but at least he was honest. I turned over his cards, just to see.

"Nothin'," I smiled. I'd won fair and square.

Shouting erupted just outside our safe little enclave. It was time to disappear.

I grabbed my cousin's arm, "Zach, you got your bike outside?" He was already on his feet, fury darkening his features and the thrill of the fight pumping in his veins. I could hear the dispute escalating in the main room, and I knew that an accident could easily turn into a bar brawl on any given night at After Dark. The last thing I needed was to be floating in a sea of testosterone, with an enticing display of flesh barely concealed. Not to mention broken glass under my shoeless feet. "Can you get me out of here?"

Zach tried to yank his arm away, annoyed. He loved the fray. But I clung on and he sensed my desperation; the fog cleared from his eyes as he looked down at me. When I held open Tristan's jacket to let him see how scantily clad I was underneath, he stepped back, his eyebrows shooting up.

"Yeah, you don't need to be here. Come on."

He helped me stuff my winnings into the little beaded handbag I had bought for the dance, and I winced as I heard a seam pop in the lining. Zach pushed me out the back door, just as Terry Finley hollered from deeper inside the bar, "Hey! We ain't finished playin'—you can't just sit in one hand."

"Yes, I can."

The back slit of my dress tore up to the zipper as I hopped onto the motorcycle behind Zach. He didn't have helmets, so I took Tristan's red silk handkerchief and wound it into a rope to tie up my hair. I held on tight to my cousin, the engine already roaring to life. Thank god, too. The wife beater looked mad. He was scowling in the doorway and his rage washed over me like a cold shower.

Just then, a fist met the back of Terry Finley's head and I didn't care if it was wrong to leave or not. "Go, Zach, go!"

We tore through the gravel parking lot, and I saw the melee was already spilling out onto the front porch. I gripped Zach's torso tighter, craving the safe, warm bed where Tristan was snuggled more than ever. My pulse was thundering, louder than the motorcycle in my veins, as we raced down the road.

When we were clear, Zach slowed and asked, "Where to? Home?"

"Um. No. You'll never guess."

He rolled to a stop and twisted in his seat to look at me. "I think I might."

I felt my cheeks burn. Who in our high school hadn't heard about my scandalous Homecoming date? "You know where the Jameson house is?" I asked, attempting nonchalance.

"The *sheriff's* house? Uh, yeah. What delinquent doesn't?"

I wondered how many times that house had been toilet-papered over the years. I looked away, not really wanting Zach's opinion.

"You sure, Meg?"

"I was invited, and very welcome to stay tonight."

"Alright, alright," he shook his head, chuckling, and he put the bike in gear. "Let's go."

We reached the valley floor and picked up speed, hurdling down the highway in a tunnel of roaring wind. I cheered him on and squeezed him with my knees to urge him faster and the engine roared louder in answer. My stomach lurched and a thrill zinged up my spine. I thought about the wad in my purse—I hadn't counted it, but I knew it was a lot. And Sleeping Beauty was waiting for me. I didn't think I'd ever felt that good.

I wasn't sure if Tristan and I would still be alone, so I had Zach drop me down the street. Sure enough, as I walked up to the house, I saw an illuminated window in the opposite corner from the master bedroom.

At least his sister had finally come home. As annoying as that was, I was glad she was safe, for Tristan's sake. I crept around the back of the house to look for an opening in the fence. The gate screeched when I eased it open, so I slid through the narrow crack and left it ajar. Neat white stepping stones lined a path around to the back, where I imagined led to the patio and swimming pool. My heart picked up its pace in anticipation, while I tried to slow my steps. I couldn't wait to cuddle in. But, as I rounded the corner, my heart slammed into my throat and my toes nearly tripped me.

No!

The undulating blue light of a TV glowed through the curtained windows of the master bedroom. He was awake. The blood drained from my face, realization dawning. My poker game hardly seemed so fun anymore. How stupid—why did I leave while he was sleeping? What did he think when he woke up to find me gone?

The glare from the pool light reflected against the glass doors, so I couldn't see what waited for me inside. I hesitated, not sure I wanted to see. Hooking a finger in the handle, I held my breath and slid the door open, relieved it was still unlocked for me.

"Please don't be too mad," I prayed silently, my eyes shut tight. I opened them and scanned the dimness, looking everywhere but where I figured he must be. The light and noise from the TV blended reality into an eerie multiverse microcosm.

He snapped it off and the remote control clattered onto the coffee table.

Silence loomed so large my ears rang.

Looking at my feet, I finally managed to say, "Hi," in a small voice.

After a grueling pause: "You know, I really didn't think you were coming back. But then I saw you left your shoes…"

I finally looked at him. He was sitting in an armchair with his legs crossed and a blanket across his lap. His hands were busy shredding a rose petal (one of many, lying tortured in front of him), his eyes were focused on my feet, and one corner of his mouth was turned up in a rueful smile. I tucked my toes in; my feet were as dirty as if I'd been playing in a schoolyard all afternoon.

"Of course I was coming back, Tristan. How long have you been awake?"

"Since right after you left." He ran a hand through his hair, then waved it in the direction of the street. "I saw you drive off with Barney in the limo."

"Oh." I pictured him sitting there awake the whole time I was gone, while I'd been imagining him blissfully unaware, curled up in cozy covers.

Jake's earlier remark about deviants knowing this house was a bitter re-crimination. So that was my crowd. "I'm so sorry I didn't take you with me, but I didn't want to wake you up and I couldn't sleep—"

"Take me with you." His tone was suddenly harsh. "Is that a joke? Take me where?"

"To the poker game, where Barney drove me."

He stared at me.

I flinched; his gaze was blue fire.

Without warning, his face split into a breathtaking smile and he collapsed back into his chair. "She went to a poker game," he said to the ceiling, then clapped his hands over his face and laughed softly.

"Why is that so funny?"

"I thought you left *with* Barney," he said into his hands, his voice muffled. He shook his head wearily and scrubbed his knuckles against his scalp.

"*With* Barney?" Oh. My face went up in flames with the knowledge of what he thought I'd been doing all that time. Not playing poker. "Are you kidding? No," I bristled. Was my reputation really that shitty? "Like I would ever do something like that. My god."

"Now I'm the one who's sorry," he said quickly, sitting up and reaching a hand towards me. "I'm not trying to insult you. I just get weird ideas when I'm jealous."

Jealous. I looked again at the torn flowers in his lap.

"You're hard to predict, you know that? Where did you find a poker game?" he asked, amazed.

"After Dark," I said with a shrug. "They always have one on Sat—"

"After Dark, the bar?" He'd stopped smiling.

"Yeah."

"You went to that shithole in the hollows, dressed like that?" His face warped into a mask of fury. "Do you have any idea how dangerous that place is? You should hear what my dad's seen there."

"Come on." I rolled my eyes and found my cuticles to be extremely fascinating.

"How could you do something that crazy?" He kept from raising his voice, but I could tell it was an effort. "And when I was supposed to be taking care of you tonight."

He rose abruptly, spilling the blanket and rose petals to the floor. As tense as a bow ready to be loosed, he paced the room in front of me. Naked limbs—perfect, tempting naked limbs—stalked past and I wished more than anything that I could just go back and erase whatever I had done to screw up our previously enchanted evening.

He stopped and rounded on me, his jaw clenched and his voice deceptively quiet. "That was on *my* watch, Meg. What would I do, if something happened to you?"

"I..."

"Huh?"

"I'm sorry," I mumbled. My chin started to tremble. I wasn't used to anyone caring what the hell happened to me. I shrank back from him, watching his chest rise and fall with his rapid breath, his eyes molten.

"Just taking off!" His volume was rising. "Didn't you think I would worry when you split?"

"I...I don't know..." Concern was foreign to me. He was right; the bar was dangerous and I knew it. But, no one ever worried whether or not I was safe. Tears sprang to my eyes and I wiped them away, totally freaked. I never cry.

Tristan softened immediately, his taught shoulders relaxing and his fists unclenching. "I made you cry?"

I stared at him, wide-eyed and silent (besides the embarrassing snuffling sounds), and then looked at my feet again. He moved close enough that I could feel the heat of his anger. It was fading, tension melting. I wanted to throw myself on him, but I what if he pushed me away?

"That's the last thing I wanted." He reached a hand up to touch my face but let it hover, tentative. A tear rolled down my cheek and he caught it with his thumb, then turned his hand to brush my jaw with his knuckles. "Please don't cry."

Then the waterworks really started.

He grabbed my shoulders and crushed me to his chest, strong arms enfolding and soft voice shushing. He stroked my hair and kissed my head and I don't know how long we stood together like that. It was long enough for me to calm down, probably longer than I'd be proud to admit.

"Well, how much did you win?" he finally asked, his voice muffled against my hair.

"Uh." Hiccup. "I don't know. Lots. The buy-in was steep, so I'm sorry but I stole your dice money," I admitted, rambling like an idiot. "But I think I doubled or even tripled it."

His chest rumbled in a laugh. "I told you that was yours."

"Well, I better get it all out now." I separated from him just enough to look him in the face. "Me and Barney polished off that cheesecake."

The corners of his lips raised, but his eyes darkened. His shoulders recommenced rigidity. "Look, Meg. I don't know what you think is going on between us." He averted his gaze.

Shit. "What do you mean?"

"I don't know." His eyes were wary.

"What did I say wrong now?"

"Not wrong, just," he shrugged and looked at the floor.

I shuffled my dirty feet. "Please, tell me."

He looked at me point blank.

Oh no, what?

"I can't have you with anyone else," he let out in a rush.

I stopped breathing. Pure pleasure, with a dose of fear, flitted through me.

"That came out wrong," he sighed, looking away into the darkness over my head. "I just mean. *I* don't want to be with anyone else. This is all really. Just. Fast. I know. Do you?"

"Do I?" Could this be real?

"Want...to be with anyone else?" he almost winced.

I had already started shaking my head before he stammered out the words. "I'm yours, Tristan."

Blatant, heart-wrenching vulnerability was etched into his features, before relief washed it away. I grabbed his face in my hands and smothered him with kisses. Someone so beautiful, so perfect, and yet so uncertain. I forgot that we all feel the same pain.

"Every girl I don't want has chased me down all my life," he said between our mouths. "But when I finally find you, you run for the hills."

"I wasn't running. That's just who I am."

"I don't understand it." He grabbed the hair at the back of my neck and balled it into a fist. He pulled me back to look at me, zeroing in so close I was dizzy. "I really don't."

"I'm sorry—"

"No. I like who you are."

And I was covered once again with his mouth, his hands, his hair, enfolded in him. I was suddenly so exhausted I could hardly keep upright any longer. Did this glorious human being just tell me...wait, what did he actually tell me? I decided I didn't care about details. I leaned towards the soft, warm bed that I had been craving since I left it.

I got tripped up in the blanket he had knocked to the floor, but he caught me easily and scooped me into both arms. "Tired out?"

My head lolled back against his shoulder. "Mmmm..."

"Yeah, I bet," he snorted. "You'll have to tell me about it sometime."

"Uh huh," I managed through a yawn.

"But not tonight."

"No, please." Please, let's forget about my devious ways tonight.

Tristan lay me down gently and helped me pull the covers up to my chin. Heavenly. He slid in behind me, all silky warm skin and firm muscles.

I felt entirely too dressed, my beaded gown scratching against soft cotton and softer skin. I sighed when I felt him unzipping the back and I almost sobbed in relief when I wriggled out of my clothes, so eager to feel him without any hindrance.

"Oh, that's too perfect," I said when our limbs were blissfully entwined again, smiling up at him.

He drew back, curious. "What's Meg short for anyway? Meghan?"

"No, Mekaela. My little sisters could only say 'Meg,' and it just stuck I guess."

"Mekaela," he said, testing my name on his lips. "Pretty."

"Yeah, whatever…"

"Like you."

"Oh. Thanks."

"I mean it."

I blushed. Why did that simple word, pretty, mean so much to me? It was so sweet, so delicate, so shy. If he would have said "gorgeous" or "sexy" I probably wouldn't have noticed. But pretty was something else.

"Do you mind if I call you that?" he whispered, resting his palm on my chest.

Could he feel my heart pounding? Hear it hammering? I think that thought made it beat even faster.

He looked at his hand, covering my heart, and smiled. "I like you, too, Mekaela. A lot."

Holy crap, he did feel it.

He leaned down and kissed the spot right over my heart.

Oh, just roll with it, *Mekaela*. No, I didn't mind one bit.

chapter ten

I climbed the steps into the school bus behind a couple of sullen guys with my head down, dreading the snarky remarks and whispers I knew were due. If there was one thing I knew well about living in a small town, it was that its citizens weren't allowed to climb up the rickety social ladders without being kicked down a rung or two in the effort.

I should have hitched a ride on Zach's bike.

But I didn't want to mess up my hair.

Silly girl.

Too late; by that time, the hated yellow school bus was my only option. As if Mondays didn't suck enough. I wrinkled my nose at the familiar smells of worn vinyl, dusty floors, morning breath, and various brands of cheap shampoo. The driver ignored me as usual and lurched the bus back along its route. I had to grab the top of a seat to keep my balance, then kept my eyes on an empty bench towards the back until I tossed my book bag in front of me and slumped in. My gaze stayed fixed outside the window. After the bus pulled out of the Southern Cove Mobile Park, I braved a look around.

Everyone was still asleep. Quiet heads bobbed in front of me with the motion of the bus. One kid nodded off, his forehead thudding against the glass window. At least that was something good about Mondays: zombies.

I leaned back, shifting to the side when a spring poked me in the kidney, and closed my eyes. I hadn't heard from Tristan since he dropped me home on Sunday, but why should I have? He brought me breakfast in bed after sleeping late (neither of us too keen on an audience with his sister and her friends), and I didn't kiss him goodbye outside my place until almost noon. That was only yesterday. And what would he have needed to call me for? All our teachers had held off on homework over the Homecoming weekend, so it wasn't like he would have called me to study or anything.

That was ridiculous anyway, he wasn't going to do homework with me—he was just pretending to be interested to be polite.

Guys simply don't call me to study.

I sighed and fingered my curls. Still damp.

I got up early that morning, before anyone else was up, to go for a jog and try calming my nerves. It hadn't worked. While I was running, the thought kept popping into my head that it had all been just a dream. Then, I'd feel like someone kicked me in the stomach and I'd have to slow down to catch my breath, my heart racing so hard it hurt. A shower hadn't soothed much either, but at least the hair product Cassie gave me worked. My ringlets behaved under my own hands, just like they had for Cassie, and they were nice and bouncy.

Unfortunately, the morning was chillier than usual and wet hair didn't help. I repressed a shiver, wrapping my arms around my shoulders and glancing down to see that my nipples were poking right through my thin tan sweater like bullets. Nice. That de-simplified the simple shirt I chose to go with plain blue jeans, in an attempt to avoid undue scrutiny that day. I smoothed the front of my sweater with my forearms, willing my breasts to simmer down. Once again, I yearned for my jean jacket; I saw it in my mind, flung to the floor in frustration when I felt the crusty dried grape jelly on its sleeve. There was no time to find anything else before I rushed out the door.

I let my head bounce against the seat—just another zombie—for the rest of the drive. I closed my eyes and tried to block my brain from the delicious details of my night and morning with Tristan. Sunday had been daydreamed away, and that only made me feel more urgent and frantic Sunday night. I'd hardly slept at all, actual dreams out of reach.

"And tired eyes are so attractive," said the nag.

Did it even matter? Would I even see Tristan or talk to him? God, I didn't have any idea what to expect.

The bus wound through several neighboring housing developments higher in the mountains, before heading down past the narrow piedmont and into the valley. Way too soon, I felt the driver turn off the main valley highway and into the parking lot of Andrew Jackson High, and my gut rolled with panic.

I thought might actually throw up.

I scanned the crowd as the cheese wagon passed parked cars, and I quickly found Tristan's forest green Jeep Cherokee. He was leaning back against the hood with his feet crossed in front of him carelessly—hair still wet, but cozy in a leather, bomber-style letterman jacket—laughing at something a friend was saying. Several of his buddies were ribbing each other and shaking their heads. One of them arched backwards to howl at a particularly funny comment.

Shit.

Shame bloomed instantly and my stomach flipped, wondering what they were laughing about. I imagined the classic jokes, "Some conquest, dude. No need to beg Meg!"

As soon as we stopped, I threw my book bag onto my back and stomped down the aisle, hopping down the steps in pairs, and then heading towards the school entrance posthaste. I trudged up the sidewalk, berating myself. What was I thinking? Me and Tristan Jameson, give me a freaking break. Just another thing I'll have to live down.

Just get to home room, just get to home—

"Mekaela!"

I nearly had a coronary.

I turned, barely daring to hope.

He was jogging towards me, mouth turned down in confusion and that little furrow in his brow—above those blue, blue eyes. I looked past him and saw his friends moving away, apparently uninterested.

"Hi," I said, my blood rushing in my ears. I was unprepared for what it would feel like to see him in the flesh again; he was even more beautiful than I remembered.

"Hey," he said with the hint of a question, then kissed my cheek. "You're freezing—your face is like ice. Where's your jacket?" Accusatory, now.

"Uh. I. Um." God, stop stuttering, Meg. "I didn't realize it was so cold when I left," I lied.

"Here." He plucked my backpack from my shoulders, took off his letterman jacket, and held it open for me. "Wear mine."

Really? Asking seemed pathetic, but I couldn't mentally assimilate this new paradigm. I managed a quiet, "Thanks."

His jacket was worn-in and toasty with wool lining, the smell of leather and Tristan rising up from inside as I snuggled into it. I held my hand out for him to return my bag, but he slung it over his shoulder, against his own backpack.

He frowned at me, reproachful. "Why'd you take the bus? I came to pick you up."

"You did? I'm sorry, you didn't have to do that."

"My girlfriend's not riding the bus, wait for me tomorrow." He slipped an arm around my waist and steered me toward the front doors. It was good someone was steering. I was adrift on a sea of screaming hormones.

Girlfriend?

"You really need to get a cell phone. Your house phone has been busy since yesterday."

"It has?"

"Yeah, I've been trying to call you."

"Oh." How thoughtless not to check; Charlie always hung up the phone wrong so the receiver stayed just off the hook.

We reached the front of the building and Tristan leaned forward to pull the handle first, stepping aside for me like the perfect gentleman.

"After you," he said when I hesitated.

As I walked through, several plump little faces crumpled in dismay, gawking openly at me and Tristan, who were obviously a pair. The girls turned to stare as we walked past. I met their gazes and grinned. I knew it was childish and catty, but I couldn't help it. Then, I turned back around to catch unbelievable hatred seething in another pair of eyes, just inside the foyer. Ashley.

Tristan ignored her.

I gulped. Holy shit. How was this gonna play out?

I was used to glares, of course. I could already feel whispers tickling up the back of my neck. But I knew Tristan wasn't used to anything like that. How would he react to it? I retreated further into his jacket like a scared turtle.

"You *want* me to pick you up, right?"

"Huh?" Was he really oblivious to the brewing melodrama all around us?

"For school," he said, a crooked smile playing on his lips. "In the mornings."

Jesus, he looked so worried. How could he not see how crazy I was about him?

"Tristan, please," I laughed, reaching up to smooth the worry line in his forehead that I was already getting used to. I smothered him with a kiss, reveling in the gasp of another passerby. I deepened the kiss and ran my hand through his hair. After I heard a grunt of disapproval from someone who could've been a teacher, I leaned back to look at his beautiful face.

His swollen lips raised in a little smile. "That was nice."

"And does that answer your question?"

His eyes were still closed in pleasure, tuning out everything but me. "Yeah."

"Okay, then. No more doubts."

He came out of his daze, gave me a lustful grin. "No."

My fingers threaded in his, I towed him towards my locker first, wanting to relieve the poor guy of dual book bag duty as soon as possible. But, I felt his hand clench when we rounded the corner, his breath catching as he came to a halt in the middle of the hallway.

"What's wrong?"

His eyes were burning with rage, fixed ahead of us. Right at my locker. "What the hell is that?"

"Oh. Great."

Someone had written "TRAMP" in dark red lipstick across the door of my locker. It was the exact hue of the dress I had worn Saturday night. Nice girls always paid attention to such details. My ears prickled with heat, but I continued on to my locker. I was instantly wide awake; humiliation is better than a cup o' Joe on a Monday morning.

I squeezed his hand, begging him to follow me, and murmured, "I'm surprised Henry didn't already catch it. He's usually faster than that."

"Someone is going to pay for that," Tristan said through clenched teeth, stalking closer, glaring at the lipstick.

"Probably won't ever find out who did it," I shrugged. My eyes slid over to him as I fumbled with the combination on my lock. At least he hadn't run yet.

"Yeah, well." He dropped my hand.

No.

Without another word, Tristan dumped my book bag at my feet and was gone. My guts went liquid. My nose tingled and I begged myself not to cry. Why was I suddenly crying all the time now, for fuck's sake? And why should he have to share in my shame anyway? Last thing I wanted to do was taint somebody so perfect.

"Crap," I choked. I couldn't let them see me cry.

I kept my eyes off the new commentary on my character, stone-faced, as my lock clicked open and I pushed the door aside. Henry would clean it later. I could do this. Just had to get through the day. I reached down for the zipper on my bag.

Oh. He left both our bags.

"Let me get that off first, Mekaela."

Tristan appeared next to me with paper towels.

"*I'm* gonna find out who did it." He slammed my locker door shut and smeared the red lipstick in a bloody gash across the door. Throwing the dirty one down, he resumed wiping with another paper towel, with about the same effect. I twisted my fingers together, not daring to look around and hoping he had brought enough supplies from the bathroom.

"You don't deserve this," he fumed, his breath starting to come fast with the effort.

"I know," I mumbled. If only he could clean away all that the graffiti meant, and the enmity behind it, too. "Can't let it bother you, I guess."

"Yes. You can."

I sighed, desperate for the chore to end.

"There. Ridiculous." Finally finished, Tristan balled the paper towels together and sent the wad soaring past several surprised freshmen. They scurried like surprised pigeons as it slammed against the inside of a trash can, echoing out of the hollow cylinder.

"Thank you," I said in the answering silence.

He turned back to me, warmth and understanding in his eyes. "No problem, darlin'."

My heart skipped a beat. High-class molasses.

I felt a smile spreading into my cheeks, but Tristan remained severe. He stood next to me, offering a scorching look of suspicion for everyone who passed by, as I opened my locker again and found the books for first period.

"I'll walk you to class," he said, taking my bag from me as soon as I zipped it up.

"Okay." I accepted his hand greedily, more relieved than I wanted to let on. The halls seemed pretty empty all of a sudden, though. No wonder.

But when I risked a glance at Tristan's face, his features were serene. His smile was easy again, the swagger replaced in his stride. He winked and I grinned—would I ever get used to how that little gesture affected me? Soaking up his confidence like a sponge, I squared my shoulders and straightened my spine. Hands clasped, we made our way through the bare corridor.

Together.

To be continued in part two of Catchpenny: Battle Ax. Find it on Amazon, and other online retailers, beginning August 1, 2015. Read on, for a sneak...

part two: battle ax

As soon as I walked through the doorway to the courtyard, I could see the group gathering in one corner—mostly guys, packed together to hide the fight from the Andrew Jackson faculty long enough to see some action.

"Shut your mouth or I'll knock the rest of your teeth out."

Oh, shit. I recognized that voice like it was my own, and the fury that laced it twisted my stomach into knots.

Another voice, higher pitched, cackled, "Let's go, Pretty-Boy."

I climbed onto a bench for a better view and saw the misleadingly scrawny Shark Powell, aptly named for his dangerous arrangement of front teeth and his habit of circling prey in a fight. He was circling Tristan. The assembled crowd was starting to roil with angst, egging on the combatants and watching the doors for threat of adult interference.

I pleaded under my breath, "Watch out, Tristan."

I wouldn't have been surprised if that creep had a knife hidden in his combat boots. I craned my neck to see inside the building, hoping for sign of some teacher bustling through the doors. "Come on come on come on!"

Scum of the earth shouted, "Alright, let's go," and, "Do it, you pussy."

I grabbed my hair and pulled hard. I turned back to the fight, cramming my fingers to my lips, but my mangled nails had already been chewed to the quick. Shark lunged and I caught my breath. But Tristan was nothing if not fast, and he ducked away easily. Then they were both circling.

I sucked in a lungful. "Crap, here we go."

Another look at the doors showed no teachers alerted yet, just more students spilling outside. I wasn't sure whether I should go get someone or not—I didn't want to leave him out there. Like that.

"—uck!"

My head snapped back to Tristan. His shouted expletive was muffled under his shirt; Shark had pulled it over his head, effectively blinding him, and then twisted it down so that Tristan was forced to hunch over.

Dirty trick! Oh please, oh please, don't break his beautiful nose.

I saw Shark's knee rising to Tristan's face.

"No!"

Tristan wrenched free and threw a solid uppercut on his way up. I heard his fist make impact with something bony.

"Alright, break it up!"

"Oh thank god," I breathed, as Mr. Davis brushed past me, shoving spectators out of the way.

Relief flooded through me, but I shook all over. I got a glimpse of Tristan's face as the guidance counselor hustled him towards the office. He was scanning the crowd, looking for me.

"I'm here," I called in a trembling voice, waving my hand high.

He flashed me his home run smile just before ducking inside the building, and then was gone. I blew out my breath in both gratefulness and disappointment—he didn't seem hurt, but I'd be eating alone. The dispersing crowd offered more than a few dirty looks in my direction. The ones who hadn't heard what started the fight (me, of course) were being filled in via whisper network. I wondered what nasty comments had been made about my supposedly loose nature to set Tristan off this time. I swallowed hard, my throat lined in sand, and looked down at my lonely lunch bag.

a note from the author

There is nothing like connecting with readers! I hope that you will join me on my website, www.sarahwathen.com. There, you will find my contact information and links to all of my social media outlets. I would love to hear from you.

And did you know that Catchpenny is a spin-off novel from my paranormal mystery series, The Bound Chronicles? Check out book one, The Tramp, for more adventures in Shirley County. Read on, for an excerpt...

the
TRAMP

BOOK ONE OF THE BOUND CHRONICLES

SARAH WATHEN

The Tramp

prologue

Summer.

"Go on. Get outta here, John." His grandma shooed him out the door with her broom like he was a stunned sparrow, trapped and ready to defile her sparkly kitchen. He was too polite to scowl, but he should have; his mother never shooed him. His dad had deposited him in Shirley County two nights before, on the first day of summer vacation, and no sooner had Dad pulled away than Grandma Pearl had snapped off the television and claimed the computer was "on the blitz."

"Set some bugs on fire or make some mud pies, but you aren't wallowing around in here."

John had no intention of wallowing anywhere, but he wasn't sure where to start roaming. The country was so different from the crowded city streets that were usually out of bounds for seven-year-olds. He set his hands on his hips and looked to his right, down a dusty dirt road that wound towards the river to the west. He had never gone that way without his mom or dad, but he knew how to find the key to their private family boat dock overlooking the rapids. The problem was he didn't want to play by himself.

"Don't go to the river, just stay around here and find another kid or something," Grandma Pearl shouted through the screen door, reading his mind.

How does she do that? It was a skill John wanted to learn. He stuffed his hands in his pockets and turned his head in the opposite direction, to the neighbors' house up the road. He knew the McBride family that lived there through stories and vague memories of holiday weekends, but he couldn't remember anyone by name. There were always plenty of kids around at family gatherings, but the house seemed pretty quiet just then. He looked at the rambling ranch house, wishing he didn't feel so weird and abandoned, when a glinting light over the white picket fence caught his eye.

Is that water from a hose? No—it was spraying crazy in all directions, like a… like a Wet Willy?

John had seen one in a commercial once. Focused on the place, he could discern faint music blaring from a radio. "Lucy in the sky-y with di-a-monds…"

Then, he heard a loud whoop and the maniacal, high-pitched laugh of a pixie.

"What the f—mmmph?" John sometimes bleeped himself. Even alone, a pottymouth just seemed too wrong. Even though pottymouths felt so good to think.

Feeling less weird, and more curious, John tramped up the road to find out what the fmmmph was going on at the McBrides's. As he neared the yard and looked through the wooden fencing, he could see a skinny girl, about his age, sporting a bright yellow and white striped bathing suit, and clomping around in red rain galoshes. John couldn't see much point in the boots; he watched her dive with complete abandon onto a flooded Slip-n-Slide, and the water sloshed out the tops of her shoes when she rose to her feet. Then, as she bounded over to dance a kind of stomping polka under the lunatic rain of the plastic-haired sprinkler, he understood. Obviously, one needed boots for such a dance.

Like a berserker, but not naked. John made a mental note to find out what female berserkers wore, if there ever were any in the Vikings lore book his dad read to him. Mesmerized by the show, John suddenly vaulted in the air and screamed like a berserker himself when a huge dog slammed against the fence. Jaws snapped and spit flew out of the creature's mouth. A hellhound!

The girl screamed and leapt across the yard toward the dog. "Randal! Down, boy," she hollered, pushing her soaked hair out of her eyes and wiping her snotty nose.

John was on his butt, in the dirt, his red Converse tennis shoes like exclamation points at the end of two jutting legs. He couldn't even think of a word to bleep. The girl shouted over the cacophony of barking dog mixed with Beatles jam, "You better move back onto the street, kid. I taught him to do this if a stranger comes up to the gate."

Street? It was a dirt path, but John scrambled up to stand with his pride in his throat. He stepped backwards a few paces until his sneakers met the packed earth of Riverbend Road. He didn't like being called a "stranger," and he didn't remember the pint-sized, water-soaked redhead. She must be a part of the McBride clan, though. In a small town everyone is tied together in dozens of ways: by a sibling or a mother or a best child-hood buddy. The city was different: everyone's disconnected even though everyone lives close together. That was one of the reasons he felt so out of place in Shirley County—he didn't know everyone who knew everyone else. John considered backtracking and going to the boat dock by himself.

The redhead was cooing at the hulk of a dog, stroking his back. The mastiff, which easily outweighed her by a hundred pounds, calmed and made low purring sounds in his throat like he was a cat ready to curl up on her lap. She straightened up to appraise her guest, her eyes roaming over him, boldly.

Her eyes were black. Weird.

She was pretty. John felt his cheeks burn and then a weird tingly feeling crept up his crotch. He shifted his weight and scratched places that didn't itch. She watched him, more comfortable in the country quiet than he could ever imagine being.

"Hi, I'm Candy," she finally belted out, with a wide, friendly smile. "This is Randal."

"Uh…I'm John." He put out his hand, starting to approach the fence again, but he snatched it back when Randal lurched forward with a slobbery warning growl. Candy had a strong grip on his collar and, in no danger herself, giggled confidently. Her laugh was gleeful—contagious—and John grinned despite himself.

"Cherry lollypop?" he asked.

Her brows knitted in confusion.

John gestured to her tangled hair, all twisted up and pinned around her head in long braids. Whoever had tried to tame it that morning had lost the battle. The ends stuck out, higgledy-piggledy, her long bangs framing her face in wild matted disarray. The effect was a perfect half-chewed lollypop on her pale slender frame. "Maybe tangerine," John reconsidered, pondering the color of her hair and cocking his head to the side—she wasn't quite a carrot top.

"Huh? Oh—candy. Ha ha, so funny." Candy mussed her uncivilized head and then pointed to his. "You're a Lemonhead, then."

Not bad. His nicely combed hair was already frizzing and curling up around his temples, rounding out his blonde head, just like the cartoon on a Lemonheads candy box. He could feel it fuzzed around his temples and he hated that. His pressed blue polo, buttoned nearly to the top, completed the look. He unbuttoned a button. They both chuckled; their hilarity gaining intensity as Candy snorted and clapped her hand to her mouth with a loud wet slap.

"Laffy Taffy," John accused.

Candy let her knees buckle, sinking to the muddy grass, and grabbing her crotch. "Stop, I'm going to pee."

"Oh—sorry." John cast around for an adult, an outhouse, something.

"Don't worry, we can wash off." She tore off across the lawn towards the sprinkler. "Come on, he won't be mean if you come through the gate."

John knew he should get soaked too after the hellhound jump scare. He shoved his hands in his pockets and shifted his damp shorts around. *Whoops.*

Randal had settled down and didn't spare him more than a passing glance as he came through the proper gate. He stripped off his polo, kicked off his shoes, and ran headlong into the Wet Willy before Candy could notice that his shorts were already wet in the one telling spot. She couldn't have noticed much, already dancing in the sprinkler, closing her eyes and singing at the top of her lungs. John leaned over and sent muddy water flying against her skinny white legs. She tackled him first, and then brought him back up to dance, her cold, water-logged hands insistent. Randal jumped in to snap at the whirling tubing, got sprayed and whipped in the face, and jumped back out ad nauseam. He tired of the water play after a while, and slouched over to blend with the wooden shaded porch. His eyes rolled back in his head and his muscular haunches twitched in a dream state. Guard dog indeed.

Candy suddenly froze, gasped, and grabbed John's arms. She held him still under the tinkling rain of the sprinkler. "Hey, wanna go look for rubies in the creek?"

"There are rubies in there?" John was surprised, but he already trusted in Candy's superior country girl knowledge of the great outdoors.

"Oh, yeah. Sapphires, too." She nodded, wide-eyed, and moved in closer to conspire, "My Uncle Pat told me he found a sapphire this big," her hands cupped to hold an imaginary goose egg, "when he was my age, and he sold it for a million dollars."

"Wow."

"I like rubies better though—they're red. Hold on, let me go put Randal inside."

She turned off the water. The wiry plastic mini-hoses collapsed to the ground as the last of the water dribbled out the end of each tiny tentacle. She meant to leave John on the porch for the quick dash inside, but her grandma insisted they both come in for a hug and a sandwich, before setting out on their expedition. John was happy to oblige, starting to feel a fondness for red himself.

After lunch, they left the big house through the back door and headed through the yard towards the dense woods. Randal stayed behind, to John's relief. The kids walked past a wooden play set, complete with slide and clubhouse, which John admired longingly. He wondered where all Candy's cousins were that day. The place seemed so quiet, not the usual bustling beehive of the large McBride family. As they climbed up a rocky narrow path, into the trees, Candy explained that one of her cousins was graduating from college that weekend and that most of the family were at the ceremony. She had complained of a stomachache, but really only dreaded the lacy dress she would have been forced to wear had she attended the party. Grandma Catherine preferred to stay home and get things ready for the inevitable family celebration at the homestead, which followed all important McBride Family events.

"Somebody has to watch Uncle Tommy, anyway," Candy remarked with a wave of her hand, referring to her uncle who even John remembered. He was large and kind, probably older than John's dad, but he seemed like a child in pre-school.

The pair grew hushed as the evergreen forest closed in around them. They stepped carefully over loose earth and around algae-covered boulders, still slippery from a recent rain, and the air felt moist and heavy as they approached the creek. John spotted a patch of bright orange mushrooms sprouting around the base of an enormous pine tree.

"Which alien planet sent those as spies?" he wondered aloud.

Delighted, Candy decided that they must find clues to lead them to the mushroom spaceship, which set in motion a competition to find the crustiest yellow lichen. No rubies or sapphires were discovered that day, but John did find a bright red ladybug that he swore bit his nose, despite Candy's protestations that "fairies" don't bite. Candy found a profusion of blue flowers with yellow sunny centers and John helped her thread them into her braids—long since tumbled loose, falling like thick ropes over her skinny shoulders. After hours of searching, they found a scummy brown crawdad that scuttled away into a deep black hole. Almost as good as an alien spacehip. The day grew warm and the afternoon hummed with contentment as the two children picked through woodsy treasures.

In what seemed like the blink of an eye, to children lost in their own invented world, the day rushed headlong into sunset. With a despondent look through the trees at the failing sunlight splashed over a nearby field, Candy announced that they had to get back before her grandma whipped her good. Proclaiming the road around would be faster than going back the way they had come, Candy led them through the trees and they emerged on the far side of the woods. Barefoot from wading in and out of the creek and scrambling sure-toed over slimy rocks, John and Candy sat in the grass just outside of the little forest, pulling shoes back on over muddy feet.

"Candy," said a deep, quiet voice.

John jumped and Candy yelped.

"Oh my gosh. You scared me, Uncle Brian," she said, grabbing her chest. John turned to see a tall thin man in faded jeans and a worn plaid flannel shirt: cuffs unbuttoned and gaping wide at his wrists. He was walking up the road towards them. "Where'd you come from?"

"Candace, you need to come with me. Right now." He was gruff and stony-eyed, expecting immediate compliance but not exactly angry.

"Am I in trouble? It's not dusk yet, we were on our way back home."

John watched her fidget and guessed she was later than she had promised to be.

"It's okay if you come now. I can get you home faster in the truck," her uncle said, smiling and jerking his thumb back over his shoulder where his old blue pick-up idled on the side of the state road, about a hundred yards away.

"In the truck?" Candy stood up and craned her skinny neck to look around him at the waiting vehicle. Its door was ajar. "What's wrong?"

He held out his hand and flicked his fingers, impatient and distracted. "Just come with me. Now."

"Okay, I guess. Come on, John," said Candy, leaning over to haul her new friend to his feet.

Uncle Brian barked, "No. Just you. Let's go—now."

"But…" Candy let go of John's hands, pink blooming across her face. "His grandma lives right next door to Grandma Catherine."

"We're not going to Grandma Catherine's. Your mom wants me to bring you home." Her uncle clenched his jaw and gestured towards the truck again.

Something was weird. Candy had told John all about staying at her grandma's house. She would have the whole family room to herself, with her brothers and all the cousins away for the night. They had talked about a sleep-over. She looked uncertainly from John to her uncle, clearly not wanting her fun weekend to end, but also not wanting Uncle Brian to be mad at her. The pick-up's engine ticked out tense seconds. John strained his vision and could just see the limp figure of another kid asleep on the bench inside.

Candy followed his line of vision and perked up. "Andy's with you?"

"Yes. Everything's fine, sweetheart," Uncle Brian said, his tone softening and his smile returning.

The smile looked forced to John.

"Okay. Well…bye." Candy dove in to embrace John, who had been standing next her with a frown. She squeezed his waist, then leaned back and shrugged, "You just follow the trail around either way. It leads you right back to your grandma's house. Or mine. It just circles the woods. Sorry." She turned to walk with her uncle, without taking his hand.

"I can find it," John said, not entirely certain that he could. But the unfamiliar trail was not what was setting his nerves on edge. That kid in the car looked more passed out than asleep; and John didn't like the way Candy's uncle smiled with his mouth but not his eyes. Creepy. He thought about saying something, but only managed to return Candy's own soft, "Bye."

John watched her walk away, her cut-off jean shorts still damp and muddy in the rump, and her coppery braids twisting down her back, trailing blue flowers with every step. She got into the cab next to her "sleeping" cousin, pinned between him and that Uncle Creepy, and waved from behind a filthy window. Her uncle slammed his door, avoiding John's gaze. Then, the ratty truck spun its wheels hard, and they peeled away off the grassy shoulder, tires squealing on the asphalt. John gasped and trotted over to the road to see them racing away in a cloud of dust.

"No…"

He sprinted home, his feet pounding the packed earth and his lungs choking on their exit.

§

"I'm sure," he told his grandmother, "Candy called him 'Uncle Brian'."

"John says it was *Brian*, not Pat, that picked her up," Grandma Pearl insisted into the phone receiver. She had been in the middle of making their usual Sunday dinner with Aunt Beth when John burst through the door. Dinner sat forgotten on the stove. "Yes, Sheriff—that's right. Candace Vale, little Candy. She must be about seven…"

John's aunt patted his hand and pushed the glass of juice towards him once more, urging, "Honey, you need to drink this. You need to calm down."

John was sure they put Benadryl in the juice to make him sleepy, but he wasn't having it. He arrived on the scene huffing and puffing, after sprinting for over a mile, but he was not in a panic. He needed to know what was happening in that nasty old truck; with that man with the oily smile. He needed to know that Candy was safe and he had a queasy feeling in his gut that she was not. His report of the strange episode had been greeted with blanched expressions from both his grandmother and his aunt. When his

Uncle Dan, who had been chatting in the den with Grandpa, heard what they were talking about he raced out the door and jumped into his jeep, rambling on his cell phone. John's cousins were loitering in the side rooms and hallways, lurking around corners and eavesdropping.

"So, you said Brian told her that you couldn't come with them? That Candy's *mom* told him to come?" Beth wrung her hands under the table. "No, that doesn't sound right…" She trailed off, beseeching her mother with her eyes.

"No," Grandma Pearl snapped. "Damnit, I know for a fact that no one in that family has seen or heard from Brian McBride in over two years. He is dead to them."

Find The Tramp: Book One of the Bound Chronicles on Amazon, and other online retailers.